The Fat Woman Mystery

Sandra Noble

Mystery
Noble

To AH.

ISBN: 1492808024
ISBN-13:9781492808022

DEDICATION

For Judi, Joan, and Janelle

ACKNOWLEDGMENTS

Thanks to Chad, Travis, Corrie, Lance, Brandy, Nicole, Joe, Frank and Sherian for their encouragement, interest and enthusiasm for this novel. And to Kathy Z. and Nicole for their proofreading skills.

CHAPTER ONE

Two hundred and eight pounds.

I stepped off the scales, waited for the numbers to roll back to zero, then stepped back on.

Two hundred and eight pounds.

Of course it wasn't really two hundred and eight pounds because it was nearly five in the afternoon. It'd been a busy day and I hadn't weighed this morning. Every fat woman knows the only time to weigh is first thing in the morning, naked, after you use the bathroom and before breakfast. By now I'd gained water weight and there was a day's worth of food stored in my body. I could subtract at least two pounds. Two hundred and six was my true weight.

Still, I was up a pound and the 'Fit Girls' would arrive at seven.

I brushed my teeth while I pondered the weight gain. The dreaded menopause was messing with my metabolism, making

my waist thicker than ever. Okay, maybe
a few too many French fries and late
night snacks were a contributing factor,
but when the hot flashes wake you at two
in the morning and you can't get back to
sleep what else are you supposed to do
besides eat? There certainly isn't
anything on television at that hour.
Maybe a few infomercials on the latest
miracle weight loss product, but who
believes that crap?

And why is it that a side effect of
all those weight loss pills is always
bowel seepage?

My cat, Ruby, jumped into the sink
as I rinsed my mouth. I adjusted the
water stream so she could get a drink
and caught a glimpse of myself in the
mirror.

Rats! Toothpaste on my boob again.

Everything ends up on my chest. I
should be running about with a bib tied
around my neck. People think fat women
all have big butts and thunder thighs,
but the truth is we come in a variety of
shapes just like skinny girls. I'm what
they call an apple, wide shoulders, a
barrel chest, lean thighs, and no ass to
speak of.

At least I don't have to get naked
in front of anyone. That's one of the
good things about being a widow. Aah,
it wouldn't have turned Harry off. My
friend Sara thinks losing Harry is the
main contributing factor to my twenty
pound weight gain this past year. She
thinks I miss him more than I realize.

A year.

Actually, it'd been a year and two months since Harry, who was never overweight, died of a massive heart attack. I'm not sentimental. The truth is, I loved Harry madly but he could be a real pain in the butt. On the other hand, I wasn't easy to live with either.

I remember one morning when we were fighting about the dirty clothes Harry had left on the floor. In exasperation he said, "You're probably right Margaret, I'm a slob, but I get tired of you ordering me around like I'm an errant teenager."

He was right. I do like things to go my way.

Money was another problem. About six years ago, when his Dad died, Harry inherited a pile of money, a source of never-ending argument between the two of us. I liked the bills paid and a fat savings account. Harry agreed that the bills should be paid, but as for saving, forget it. He wanted to travel, eat lobster, and drink champagne. He would have gone through that cash like a blow torch through dry leaves, but I insisted we invest for our old age.

Poor Harry.

He was only fifty-five when he died and never did get to have fun with his money. I learned my lesson. For once Harry was right. Better enjoy yourself today 'cause you may not have a future. Good thing my father-in-law's dead. I didn't fit into his idea of a well-behaved wife. Knowing I ended up with everything would have killed him.

If I could snap my fingers and have Harry back, I'd snap in a heart-beat, but there are perks to being a widow. I loved the years that Harry and I were raising our family. That time had incredible joys, but after decades of rolling out of bed at some ungodly hour and scrambling to get myself, the kids, and Harry fed and out the door, leisurely mornings are pure delight. I like being accountable to no one but myself, and having the only say when it comes to finances.

Every season of life has a new set of perks.

I love Wednesdays.

The Fit Girls meet Wednesday evenings at my house. I retired when Harry died, after working as the high-school librarian for nearly thirty years. My kids are grown and living in other states, and since I don't have a husband to consider, it's easiest to make my place Fit Girls headquarters.

Everyone brings a sandwich and baked chips and we sit around my dining room table to share the evening meal. If I feel like it I call everyone to say I'm cooking.

Tonight I'm cooking. We're having green beans from Sara's garden, spiced with Cajun seasonings and garlic, and cooked in fat free chicken broth along with onion and a small potato each.

Earlier I seasoned a lean pork tenderloin roast with rosemary and put it in the crock pot. For dessert I made instant sugar free banana pudding, adding a few banana slices and a dollop of low fat Cool Whip.

A great meal for about six hundred calories.

#

Karen arrived first. She's thirty-eight, fifteen years younger than me but we've been friends for ages. We met when we were both serving on the Christmas Tree Gala committee.

At the time Karen was a big girl and we went on the Herbal Life diet together. We called it Herbal Death. It involved popping pills four times a day. Lord knows what was in them. I think the saleswoman said vitamins, but there had to be another ingredient because they sure made me talk fast and my house had never been so clean. Herbal Death started Karen and me on the diet trail hand in hand.

Karen's single right now but she's had two husbands. She loves bad boys: the guys who drink too much, have a little swagger to their walk, and enjoy an occasional brawl.

Karen's lost seventy-five pounds over the past two years, and thanks to her Slimfast, and a change in her eating habits, she's kept it off. She sells real-estate and does a fine job at it. She says being a fat teenager forced her to develop personality, which is useful in sales.

Even when she was fat Karen had an hourglass figure. Her hips and bust are in balance and her waist is small. She keeps her blonde hair short, and her face has a Drew Barrymore perkiness that brings a smile to your heart. Now and then a few pounds creep up on her when she's stressed, but Karen just goes back to using Slimfast for breakfast and lunch, and hitting the treadmill double time until she's on track again.

Always the klutz, Karen caught her sleeve on the latch as she swept through the door. "Hi Margaret, dinner smells great," she said, as she casually freed her sweater. "I love it when you cook. I swear, when I eat here I'm down a pound the next morning. What can I do to help?"

"Nothing. The table's set and the food's nearly ready. Did you have a good week?"

She followed me to the kitchen so I could oversee dinner. "I sold the Saber house today," she said.

I rewarded her with a big hug and a bigger smile. "Good job. You'll do all right on that sale. It's a nice house."

Karen took a seat at the drop leaf table to keep out of the way as I zipped around taking care of the last details of the meal. "I wish my personal life was going as well as work," she said. "My sister's driving me up a wall. Mom lost twenty pounds on that fat binding diet pill, now Jean Ann's decided to try it."

As I lifted the crock pot lid to
check the roast, my face was enveloped
with rosemary-infused steam. It was
ready to serve. I turned to Karen, "How
does that pill work?"

"It's supposed to prevent some of
the fat from being absorbed."

"That should work."

I put the roast on the platter and
dished up the vegetables as Karen went
on with her lively chatter.

"I just worry because Mom gave her
the book to read but Jean Ann thinks she
knows all about that diet pill from some
article she read in the paper, so she
hasn't bothered to read any of the
instructions. If you don't eat low fat
you can lose control of your bowels.
Jean Ann thinks she can eat anything she
wants and pop one of those pills to get
rid of it. She's going to end up on the
pot all day."

I chuckled. *Here we go again with
the bowel seepage*, I thought. I said,
"I've done some dumb things on diets
too. I remember when I tried Atkins.
Just like Jean Ann, I thought I knew all
about it. I ate huge amounts of meat
and polished off a bag of pork rinds in
front of the television every night,
then wondered why I was the only one in
the world who couldn't lose weight on
Atkins."

Karen sighed, "Yeah, and when I
think about it, if I had to be married
to Albert, shutting yourself in the

bathroom all day wouldn't be a bad thing. My brother-in-law is so whacked."

I searched through the utensil drawer for a serving spoon and thought about Albert. "I'll agree that Albert's not right in the head," I said. "As for Jean Ann's diet denial, it's funny, but understandable."

Karen puffed out an exasperated sigh and sat back in her chair. "I know I should be more understanding, especially when it comes to dieting, but between Jean Ann's diet and her complaints about Albert's gambling habits" — Karen sliced through the top of her spiky blonde hair with the flat of her hand — "I've had it up to here."

I grinned, enjoying the drama of Karen's statement, but if I'd known just how much Albert would affect my life over the next few days, it would've wiped the smile from my face.

I heard the back door open and looked up to see Sara. "Is it safe to come in?" she asked as she came through the door. "Karen sounds angry with someone."

Karen smiled, happy to see our friend. "I'm just ranting about my sister and brother-in-law again."

"Come on in, Sara," I said. "Dinner's ready to put on the table."

#

We've always held Fit Girls membership to four. Right now we're short a member because Angela moved to

Florida. The girls are picky about filling her spot, so I was a little concerned. I'd promised Cindy Waveland I'd put her name up. Cindy's a dark-haired beauty in her early thirties, married to Grant Waveland. Grant's a successful lawyer and he and Cindy are two of Alta Grove's beautiful people.

Cindy moved to town when she was hired to teach music. Once hired, people seldom quit working for the Alta Grove school system. Friendships and alliances can exist for decades, making it difficult for a new employee to find their niche. When I extended a hand of friendship, Cindy adopted me as her mentor, but as much as I liked Cindy, I wasn't sure she was a good Fit Girl candidate.

Fit Girls have special attributes: we can keep our lips zipped about what we hear in meetings, a sense of humor is a must, and we share a common problem with food. While Cindy has no problem keeping her mouth shut, she's a little on the serious side, and I doubted her mere fifteen extra pounds would sway Karen or Sara. Cindy would be no shoo-in.

We don't follow "Robert's Rules of Order," but we have found a comfortable routine for Fat Girl gatherings. After we ate and cleared the table, we took our walk and then gathered in the front parlor for the meeting. Ruby, her belly pouch flapping from side to side, jogged across the room to join us. She purred, rubbed her cheek against my ankle, then took her place between Karen and Sara on the sofa.

We start with our weight, although we don't *have* to tell what we weigh. We believe that's nobody's business but our own.

"I'll start," Sara said, "because I've had a great week. I've lost three pounds!"

While Karen has a few rough edges, Sara is the epitome of a lady. She's our youngest member at twenty-eight. She has a pear shape, epitomized by narrow shoulders, broad hips, and a fluffy body.

We congratulated her on her weight loss, and then Karen announced, "I'm down too. I've lost the two pounds I gained on vacation and I'm back to my goal weight."

They looked expectantly at me, smiles on their faces, waiting for more good news.

I hated putting a damper on the weight loss roll, but I fessed up. "I'm up a pound."

Sara's face changed to kindly concern. "Don't worry about it, Margaret. You've had a lot of stress this year."

"Yeah," I agreed. "Twenty pounds of stress. If I don't get a handle on this I'm gonna regain all fifty pounds."

Sara tucked a tendril of shiny strawberry blonde hair behind her ear.

"That won't happen," she said. "I can tell because you're getting back to your old self. The house is cleaner, you're starting to exercise again, and you're spending more time on your appearance."

I raised an eyebrow. I couldn't remember the last time I'd even had my hair trimmed.

Karen jumped in to help bolster my self-esteem. "She's right. Just getting out of your pajamas before it's time to go back to bed is an improvement."

Don't ask me why, but their attempts to cheer me up kind of irritated me. "You guys always act like Harry's death devastated me. I'm fine."

Sara looked at me with sorrowful eyes. "We understand how much you're missing Harry. You don't have to pretend with us."

Time to change the subject. Sara has great empathy for people and too much sympathy always makes me cry. "You both know Cindy Waveland," I said. "She's heard me talking about Fit Girls and wants to join."

Silence.

I tried again. "I know Cindy doesn't fall into what any of us would call the 'fat' category, but she took up baking and gained weight recently, and she's concerned she won't be able to hold the line."

Silence.

I waited them out. Finally Karen spoke.

"I've always been comfortable in

Fit Girls because I can talk about
things people who start out ten or even
twenty pounds overweight would never
get. If I told Cindy I fell off the
wagon while I was in Waterloo and
stopped at Burger King for a whopper and
fries, then at Dairy Queen for a
chocolate cone, and later at the bakery
for a cream horn, she'd be disgusted.
Hell, even I'm disgusted when I do that
crap, but I trust you guys to at least
understand."

Sara nodded. "Cindy is a
sweetheart. I've worked on community
projects with her several times. But I
wouldn't dream of telling her I've
poured water over food before dumping it
in the garbage so I wouldn't dig it out
to eat later."

The Fit Girls were only saying what
I knew was truth. "We're agreed then.
I'll give Cindy our decision."

#

The next morning, when I came
downstairs, I paused at the first
landing, as I often do. I've lived in
my house for thirty years, but I have
never gotten over the beauty of the
woodwork in the pocket doors, or the
graceful curvature of the staircase.

Most the houses in town, of the
Victorian era, have oak woodwork, and
oak is beautiful, but the abundant wood
in my home is butternut. Butternut's
darker than oak, but not nearly as dark
as walnut or as red as mahogany. I like
this unique feature of the house, and I

let myself appreciate the foyer before I continued on to the kitchen.

Like many kitchens in old houses, mine's too small. I was able to eke out just enough space for a drop leaf table so Harry and I could eat in the kitchen. Any time the kids are home or I have company, we move to the dining room.

As I put breakfast together I repeated the mantra I'd started while still in bed.

Today I'll stick to my diet. Today I'll leave the sugar alone. Today I'll eat healthy.

I made oatmeal and Ezekiel bread toast with cashew nut butter for breakfast. I was following a no sugar, no white flour diet, and tried to include protein, a veggie or fruit, and a whole grain carb with each meal. It's not as simple as all that, but that's the nutshell version.

I was also using organic foods, which can be expensive. I fight the cheap part in me to spend the money it takes to buy healthy food. It's hard to understand why it costs more to buy the can of soup with less salt.

After breakfast I got out of my pajamas sooner than usual because I'd promised Cindy we'd go for a morning walk. I wasn't looking forward to seeing her because I'd have to tell her the Fit Girls had turned down her request to join.

I went to the porch to wait. My street, Ascension, is in one of the

oldest areas of Alta Grove. Huge,
hundred-plus years-old sugar maples line
both sides of the road, shading
substantial areas from the roasting
summer sun.

The houses on my block were built
in the late 1800s. They're decorated in
painted lady style and set on large
lots. My Queen Anne sat on a corner.
It's painted in monochromatic greens
that blend with the green foliage of the
trees, the grass, and the row of old-
fashioned snowball bushes along the
front of the porch.

It's a cool inviting look that
belied the heaviness of the morning's
air. By noon the heat would be intense,
sending anyone with half a brain inside
with the air conditioning.

I waved as Cindy, pushing two year
old Angie in her stroller, neared my
house. Her dark hair gave a healthy
bounce with each stride of her long tan
legs. She was wearing a sleeveless
print blouse. I noticed the definition
of her bicep muscles and fought off the
mini invasion of envy. I never wore
sleeveless. First, my arms were too
fat, and second, despite lifting soup
cans to tone my arms, I was developing
bat wings.

I greeted Cindy, and fussed over
Angie before we fell into step.

Walking in Alta Grove is a social
event. People watering their flowers
call out greetings, other walkers and
bikers pass with smiles and hellos, so

we'd nearly reached the fairgrounds before Cindy mentioned Fit Girls.

"Did you talk to the girls about letting me join?" she asked.

I made my voice cheery. "Yes, and it's the old good-news bad-news thing. The good news is you aren't enough overweight for Fit Girls membership. It's also the bad news."

Cindy stopped walking. Her shoulders slumped as she looked at me. "I'm so disappointed," she said. "I really think your diet group's the answer."

"I know that's how you feel," I said gently, "but your weight problem isn't the same as ours, and you should be grateful for that."

She adjusted the stroller's canopy to keep the sun out of Angie's eyes, and we begin walking again. "I just don't understand."

"I know," I said. "That's why Fit Girls isn't the place for you. Cindy, have you ever polished off a bag of chips when you weren't even hungry?"

"Of course not."

"Have you ever driven through a fast food place on the way home from work, then sat down to dinner with the family like you'd never eaten that burger and fries?"

Cindy laughed as she tilted the stroller back to lift it over a curb. "I'd get sick if I ate that much."

"That's what I'm trying to explain. All the Fit Girls have either done those things or something similar. Our drive to eat is different than yours."

"But I'd so pinned my hopes on the group's help to get me back in shape."

I could hear her struggle to hold back the tears. "You don't need Fit Girls," I said. "Join the health club and give up baking. I bet your weight's back to normal within three months."

We walked in silence for a few minutes before turning back toward my house. Cindy looked straight ahead, her hands white from the tightness of her grip on the stroller handles. Without looking at me, she asked, "You remember Kitty Samuels?"

I laughed. "How could I possibly forget her? She was the office vamp."

"And Grant's girlfriend when we first met."

"It didn't take him long to break it off with Kitty after he met you."

Cindy stopped walking and looked at me. "I think Grant's seeing her again."

If Grant was messed up with another woman, especially Kitty, he was an idiot. I was stunned, but after thinking about it for a few seconds, I rejected the possibility. Grant was too concerned over appearances to put his reputation in jeopardy.

"What even put that idea in your head?" I asked.

Cindy looked away, struggling with her emotions, and then bravely met my eye. "Lately Grant's been secretive about some of his phone calls. His

voice inflection changes when I walk in.
The other night, when he answered the
phone, he got a funny look on his face,
and then moved to another room to talk."

Angie fussed, growing impatient
with the pause of motion, so we started
walking again. Grant isn't among my
favorite humans, but I didn't want to
string him up without due consideration.
"Grant is a lawyer," I said. "I'm sure
he gets a lot of confidential calls."

"These calls are different."

We passed the Gleason house and
Martha called a cheery good morning. I
waved absently and Cindy and I kept
walking and talking.

"Did you talk to Grant about your
feelings?"

"After he got one of those strange
calls I asked if he was having an
affair. He denied it, but … oh
Margaret, I hate to admit this, but I
just had to know…." She tilted the
stroller to its back wheels to navigate
the curb, and then looked at me with
tears brimming in her eyes.

"Hate to admit what?" I urged.

"After Grant fell asleep I checked
his cell phone. He'd been talking to
Kitty. There must be something going on
between them. Why else would he be so
evasive about it?"

I was beginning to understand why
Cindy was stressed. If I'd found Harry
talking to another woman and covering it
up, I'd have been throwing dinner plates
at his head, but it wouldn't help Cindy

if I shared that thought. I kept my
demeanor calm.

"Did you tell him you knew he was
talking to Kitty?"

"Yes, I woke him up. I thought I
could bring him to his senses. I threw
Kitty in his face and threatened divorce
and we ended up in a huge argument.
Grant said he'd go for full custody of
Angie if we ever divorced."

I thought, *That piece of crap*, but
I said, "I'm sure he didn't mean it. He
was angry and people say ugly things
when they're mad."

"Maybe. Later he did apologize.
He said he was talking to Kitty because
they had unfinished business."

That was a relief. That made
sense. "There you are," I said. "She's
seeing him about a legal matter. If it
bothers you too much, ask Grant to have
her use another attorney."

"I did, and he said this was
something he had to take care of
himself. It's driving me crazy. What
if they are having an affair? What if
he's planning to leave me and take
Angie?"

"He can't take Angie. You're a
good mother."

Cindy lowered her voice. "I've
never told you this, but after Angie was
born, when Grant told everyone I'd taken
the baby to spend time with my parents,
it wasn't quite true. Angie did go to
my folks, but I had a terrible case of
post-partum depression and was

hospitalized for two weeks."

I hid my surprise and tried for nonchalance. "Post-partum depression is pretty common, and besides, people are more open-minded about mental illness these days. It may not be as bad as you think."

"It sure won't help. Especially when you consider how prominent Grant's law firm is in McCall County. Any lawyer I'd hire would pale in comparison to Grant's."

"You're getting worked up over a divorce when you don't even know Grant's having an affair."

"It's the not knowing that's making me crazy."

"Then hire a detective and find out," I blurted.

Cindy shivered. "I've actually thought about that, but hiring a detective seems so sleazy."

"I don't know much about these things," I said, "but I saw a Lifetime movie where this woman was trying to get the goods on her husband and she followed him herself."

She laughed. "Margaret, sometimes you get the wildest ideas."

But events got a lot wilder than anything I could've dreamed up.

CHAPTER TWO

Two-hundred and seven pounds. It was only Friday and I was already down a pound.

Relief.

I'd be mortified if I had to report a gain two weeks in a row. With buoyant spirits I dressed and zipped through the morning pet chores. I refreshed Ruby's food and water, scooped out the litter box, then took her to the front porch and brushed her coat to a high sheen.

Ruby put up with the grooming for as long as she could, then she flicked her tail in warning and thanked me for my diligence as a pet owner by trying to nip my wrist.

"All right, girl. I got the message."

I scooped Ruby up in my arms and we went back inside. I emptied the dishwasher, then went to the parlor to straighten the room. Books and magazines were strewn about my favorite chair, and the desktop was a mess, covered with the the remnants of paying bills.

Guilt nipped at me like gnats on a humid summer evening. I'd always blamed any household untidiness on Harry. Now that I was alone I understood how much of that disorder was mine. I let regret sweep through me, took a cleansing breath, and finished the housework so I could meet Sara uptown for coffee.

#

Sara's a beautiful woman. Even in my youth I doubt I ever looked so fresh. Her strawberry blonde hair was pulled back into a pony tail; curly wisps framed her face. But her green eyes were the best thing about her today, because she was wearing a light green blouse. Sara still carries a lot of extra weight, but I thought she was the prettiest woman in the room.

Sara has two kids. Josh is five and Emily is seven. She'd been driving them into town for swim lessons. After she'd drop them at the pool we'd meet at the Main Street Coffee House.

She waved when she saw me. I waded through tables, fielding greetings from friends, to join her at our favorite place toward the back of the shop. It gave us a good view of who was out and about. Between the two of us we're related to half the town.

Happy chatter and bits of laughter floated around the room, melding with the aroma of cinnamon and fresh-ground coffee. I love the smell of coffee. I associate it with my grandmother's house and waking to the perking of the coffee pot, but I never acquired a taste. I ordered non-fat Chai tea. Sara asked for straight coffee.

"Good thing you're here to keep me on the straight and narrow or I'd be ordering cookies to go with my tea," I said.

Sara grinned. "I know what you mean. Since it's Friday I'm fine, but I really have to keep busy Wednesdays or I sabotage myself. After I get on the scales for my official meeting weight, I tell myself there's a full week ahead to undo damages, so if I'm going to cheat this is the day to do it."

I spied a sack of produce on the chair next to her. "How's the garden doing?"

"Great. This bag's yours. I picked green beans, cucumbers, onions and carrots for you this morning," Sara said. "Remind me when we leave or I'll end up taking them back home."

Sara is the quintessential farmer's wife. She and Bruce live in the same house his grandparents built when they first bought the farm over a hundred years ago. Sara and Bruce were high-school sweethearts. They married young, but I think they'll last. They have the same goals in life and Sara loves country living.

Our drinks came and Sara took a tentative sip of the hot brew then set it aside to cool. "Thank goodness I had an excuse to leave the house this morning. Mom came by. She likes to check up on my diet.

I gave her my full attention because there's nothing I enjoy more than hearing stories about Sara's mom. I felt my lips curving into a smile.

"First, Mom said I looked like I'd lost more weight. Then she squinted her eyes, stared at me, and declared it wasn't weight loss, but my outfit was flattering to my shape."

I couldn't help it. I laughed. "You have to keep a sense of humor about it," I said. "She doesn't mean to put you down. She's just overanxious about your weight. You should hear some of the things my dad said to me when I was a kid."

Sara pushed a stray curl from her eyes, "I doubt he could top my mom."

I think I like hearing Sara's mother-daughter stories because it's good to know there are other parents who are as clumsy as my father was when it came to rearing an overweight child. Maybe Sara would feel the same. I decided to give her an example.

"When I was a prom queen candidate, Dad told me not to get my hopes up because fat girls are never elected queen."

"Were you?" Sara sat up in her chair expectantly.

"Nope. I came in dead last."

Sara's fine green eyes expressed her concern for me. "He shouldn't have said it anyway."

"In an odd way I think he was

trying to protect my feelings," I said. "Making sure I didn't get my hopes up."

I heard a loud thump toward the front, then the scraping of chair legs on the wooden floor. Coffee house patrons popped out of their chairs. I stood to get a better view.

"Call 911," someone called out.

It was Hazel Minnert, Albert's stepmother, on the floor. She started to get up. June Mason, the Avon lady, cautioned her to stay put, but Hazel was determined to get to her feet, so June helped her.

"Please, don't call the ambulance," Hazel said, her voice quavering, "I'll be fine."

I worked my way through the crowd to the front of the shop. "Hazel," I said, "if you don't want an ambulance, will you let me take you to your doctor?"

Hazel was relieved for the suggestion. "That'd be fine."

Everyone went back to their seats, glad to know Hazel would be cared for, and that they could go back to their visiting and coffee.

Sara hurried to us, bag of veggies in hand. "Do you need me to go along?"

"Who knows how long we'll have to wait to see the doctor, and you have to pick up the kids soon. I can handle it."

Sara nodded. "I'll drop the garden stuff at your house and call Jean Ann and Albert. They can meet you at the doctor's office."

#

By the time we pulled into Doctor
Hepple's parking lot, Hazel was better,
but she was probably eighty, an age
where you shouldn't take your health for
granted. She wasn't a frail woman, but
she looked less robust than usual after
her fall. The bump on her forehead was
growing.

"Did you trip on something?" I
asked.

"No. Suddenly I felt weak and just
went down. I've had some digestive
problems," Hazel whispered. "Di-ar-
rhea."

She put a hand to her chest. Her
voice was normal when she spoke again.
"It's made me a little woozy. I saw
Doctor Hepple last week and he said I
had the flu, but this has gone on too
long to be the flu."

She was trying to be brave, but I
could see the worry in her pale blue
eyes. "It won't hurt to be checked
out," I said.

"It's probably nothing. People my
age get touchy stomachs."

I got out of the car to go around to
help Hazel just as Jean Ann and Albert
Minnert's green pickup pulled in beside
us. Albert jumped out almost before his
vehicle had come to a full stop.

He was well over six feet, big
everyplace, but wider at the hips.
Harry always said Albert was built like
a ketchup bottle. "I'll handle this,"

Albert said.

I was taken aback by his tone. "That's fine, Albert. I was just trying to help out."

He jerked Hazel's car door open. "Didn't I tell you to stay home? You saw the doctor just last week."

Jean Ann reached his side. Even though she was considerably overweight, she seemed small next to her overbearing husband. Her speech was hesitant. "Hazel's not getting better, Albert. Maybe she should see Doctor Hepple?"

"It's a waste of time and money," Albert snapped.

Jean Ann tried for a conciliatory tone. "You're probably right." She patted his arm. "But since we're already here it couldn't hurt for the doctor to see her."

Albert started to argue but Jean Ann soothingly stroked his arm. "I think Hazel could use a wheelchair."

She steadied Hazel while Albert wordlessly went for the chair. "Thanks, Margaret," she said. "I'll be sure the doctor sees her."

I nodded. "You might want Doctor Hepple to look at her head too. She bumped it when she fell."

I gave Hazel a little hug and left Jean Ann to handle everything. No wonder the woman ate pork rinds. Albert was a pain in the ass.

#

At fifty-three I'm the granddame of the Fit Girls, but when it comes to

being fat, age has no bearing. If
you're eight years old or a hundred,
your feelings and experiences of growing
up fat are comparable. That's the glue
that binds us. After our walk and
meeting, the Fit Girls settled into the
parlor for a gab-fest.

I sighed with contentment.

I watch TV in the living room, but
when company comes the parlor's the
perfect room. It's not a large room so
when everyone's seated we're drawn
close, which invites conversation. I
painted the walls a warm dark mustard to
complement the yellow in the stained
glass window. Rose Johnson, who owns
the hardware store, tried to talk me out
of it, but I insisted it was the color I
wanted.

I'm no interior decorator, but in
this case I made a stellar choice. In
the morning sunlight glows brightly
through the yellow-stained glass fleur-
de-lis in the upper window and warms my
heart. In the evening, the colors
soften, giving mellow comfort at the end
of a day.

Karen sat in one of the wing backs,
feet curled under her butt. She patted
the edge of her chair inviting Ruby to
join her. "I've been feeling guilty
about turning Cindy down for membership.
How did she take it?"

"She was disappointed," I said.
"Her marriage is struggling and she
thinks getting back into pre-baby
condition will make Grant take more

notice of her."

Sara's face mirrored her inner kindness. "I'm sorry to hear that." She paused, as though wondering if she should say more.

Karen pushed. "What do you know?"

"I haven't mentioned it to anyone. I don't want to start any unfounded rumors, but I've been worried about something. I was in Cindy's neighborhood last week visiting my sister. We were sitting on the stoop, and Kitty Samuels drove by the Waveland house twice. Real slow. I remember thinking Kitty was up to something." She blushed. "Kitty may have had a good reason to be watching the Waveland house. Really, I don't know anything about it."

"With Kitty you do know," Karen said, with assurance. "She's always in some kind of jam and it usually involves a married man." She rolled her eyes. "Men are such fools. I can't imagine screwing around with Kitty when a class act like Cindy is waiting at home."

I was alarmed at the path the conversation was taking. The last thing Cindy needed was to have all of Alta Grove dishing over her marriage. "I think Sara's thoughts about keeping this quiet are good," I said. "If Grant is cheating, he and Cindy will have a better chance of putting their marriage back together if they don't have the town's gossip to deal with. It wouldn't be the first marriage to survive an affair."

Karen agreed. "My sister is a good example of that. Albert had a fling while he was in his mid-life crisis and Jean Ann forgave him."

I shook my head in wonderment. "You mean she had a good excuse to dump Albert and didn't do it?"

Karen and Sara laughed.

"No accounting for taste," Karen said. "Say, I meant to thank you for helping Hazel Friday morning."

Sara sat forward in her chair. "That's right. How's she doing?"

"Doctor Hepple says she needs to watch what she eats. No spicy foods and to eat more fiber, but he's such a quack. I wish she'd get a second opinion," Karen said.

"Me too," I added. "But I'm not sure Albert will allow it. He wasn't happy about Hazel going to the doctor."

Karen let out an exasperated sigh. "He's such a control freak. He told Jean Ann that Hazel keeps leftovers too long and it's giving her food poisoning."

"That's possible," Sara said. "I know my great-grandmother was raised during the depression, and she wouldn't waste a crumb. She used to wrap the last teaspoon of any vegetables left from dinner and freeze it in a bag filled with scraps of meat or veggies. When she made vegetable soup it all went in the pot."

Karen rubbed her thumb over her

lips and thought before she spoke.
"Hazel is careful about waste, but Jean
Ann and Albert have been eating at her
house at least once a week for years.
They've never gotten sick. I think her
food's safe."

She lowered her voice to a
conspiratorial tone. "I'll tell you what
is worrying me. Albert's been going
over to Hazel's and looking through her
refrigerator. He says he's tossing old
food so she won't get sick."

Sara stiffened her back. "What? Now
that is weird."

Karen nodded. "I think it's weird
too, and now I'm wondering if he's going
over there to put something *in* Hazel's
food."

The conversation had officially
entering the twilight zone. *"Doo doo do
doo. Do doo do doo,"* I sang. Karen and
Sara gave me exasperated looks. "Now
why on earth would Albert want to harm
Hazel?" I asked. "She's been a great
stepmother. She's always treated Albert
nice, even if he is nuts."

Karen waggled an index finger at
me, "Because he needs the money. Albert
thought he'd come into some cash when
his dad died, but everything went to
Hazel. Now he has to wait until Hazel
dies to see any of it. Albert's her
only heir."

Sara's eyebrows rose. "Gambling.
Right?"

"Bingo," Karen said. "Albert's at
the casino five days a week. Jean Ann

borrowed money from me to pay the electric bill last month. They were going to turn it off. Bill collectors are calling all the time and she's frantic."

I tilted my head to the ceiling, praying for a return to sanity, then I tried to reason with Karen. "If you *really* believed Albert wanted to hurt Hazel, you'd tell the authorities."

"I can't do that. How can I tell Jean Ann I think her husband's trying to kill his stepmother? I don't have a shred of evidence."

Sara put her hand to her cheek and turned to me. "We have to do something. What if Karen's right? If something happens to Hazel we'll be guilty too."

I wasn't convinced Albert wanted to kill Hazel. It was more like I was being swept up in a pretend adventure. Or maybe I just wanted to come to life again after a year of mourning. Or even that Lifetime movie I'd told Cindy about. All I know are the words that came out of my mouth.

"We should stake-out Hazel's house."

CHAPTER THREE

The morning after our Fit Girl meeting, still in my pajamas, I went to the porch to water the hanging petunia baskets. For once the Iowa humidity had fallen below a sultry rainforest level. The sun's rays were magic wands bedazzling the dew on the grass. I pulled my shoulders in as a thrill of appreciation for a perfect morning ran through me.

Breakfast on the porch seemed the best way to celebrate a perfect day. I went to the kitchen and filled a tray with a bowl of Grape Nuts, an orange, a piece of Ezekiel bread toast with butter churned from cows free of hormone injections or antibiotics, a mug of hot tea, and a cloth napkin.

Ruby knew I was up to something and followed my every move with round yellow eyes. When we got to the screen door I couldn't resist her pleading mews and let her join me on the porch for breakfast. That was a mistake. Between the beauty of the morning and my joy in the food, I lost track of Ruby.

"Ms. O'Brian."

The voice was deep and serious. I

slowly brought my eyes up to meet the gaze of my new neighbor, John Gildenbond.

"That cat of yours is digging in my flower bed again."

Uncomfortably aware I was still in my fuchsia and lime green striped PJ's, I set the breakfast tray aside and rose. "I'll get her, Mr. Gildenbond."

I left him standing on the porch steps and went next door to gather Ruby. Unfortunately I didn't reach her before she'd taken a dump in John Gildenbond's daylilies.

"Oh Ruby, we're in trouble now."

I made a dash to my back door, put Ruby inside, hurried to the garage for a shovel, and just as I was coming out of the garage saw Gildenbond headed my way.

My neighbor is nearly as good looking as he is ill-tempered. At seven-thirty in the morning he was impeccably dressed in knee-length khaki shorts, and I must say, his legs were great: muscular and tanned. He was a couple inches taller than me, maybe five-ten. The yellow polo shirt he wore was pristine, not a single stain. Every strand of his silvery hair was in place.

I wasn't even wearing slippers.

I looked down at my cherry-red toenails, wishing all two-hundred and seven pounds of me could disappear.

"I'm afraid Ruby has left a deposit in your flowers. I'll take care of it," I said.

"Ms. O'Brian, this is hardly the

first deposit that cat's made. You can imagine how distasteful it is to be weeding the flower bed and come across one of her calling cards."

Gildenbond's forehead wrinkled as his eyes narrowed. "The leash law in this town isn't just for dogs."

I hate it when I'm so wrong I didn't have an answer. All I could do was to stand in the driveway barefooted, in my pajamas, hanging my head like a teen-aged girl being scolded by her father for leaving her room a mess.

Gildenbond sure knew how to take the glow off a beautiful morning.

#

My cereal was soggy when I got back to the porch, so I picked up the tray and went inside.

The phone was ringing. It was Karen. "Albert has a fireman's meeting tonight at eight. I think we should be at Hazel's by nine in case he drops by."

"We're really going to stake-out Hazel's?" I asked.

"Someone has to do something," Karen said. "The more I think about it, the more I realize how desperate for cash my son-of-a-bitch brother-in-law is. My poor sister. I swear I'll never get married again."

I smiled. Of course Karen would marry again. The next man who swept through Alta Grove on a motorcycle would get in her blood like sugar in a Dunkin' Donuts addict's veins.

"Jean Ann called when I got home

35

from Fit Girls last night," Karen said. "She was crying. They're three house payments behind and the bank's threatening to foreclose. And get this. Albert told Jean Ann not to worry."

Karen's voice took on an ominous shade. "He told her he has a plan that will take care of all their worries."

Anxiety closed in around my heart. What if Karen wasn't being dramatic? What if Hazel was actually in danger? "Maybe we should call the police," I said.

"And say what? We'll sound like nitwits. Besides, my sister loves that creep. If we're wrong, she'd never talk to me again. I have to be sure Albert's actually putting something in the food."

"Okay. I'm in," I said.

"Good. Sara's picking us up at eight forty-five."

"Do you think Albert will recognize Sara's car?"

"We're going incognito. Sara's borrowing her dad's Chrysler. And Margaret, bring that camera Harry gave you," Karen said. "And wear black."

#

When I was younger I'd read that dark colors were slimming, so all my clothes were navy blue, brown or black. It made me feel like I could blend into the background so no one would notice how big I was. However, when I went through my *Big is Beautiful* stage, I tossed all the drab clothing and replaced it with colors and floral prints.

I searched through my closet for something left from my dark ages, but all I found was a pair of black stretch-pants my daughter had forgotten when she'd visited last month. Getting them on was like pulling on pantyhose a size too small.

I found a big hooded sweatshirt in Harry's closet, and when I looked in the mirror I saw a barrel on two toothpicks. I sighed and felt even more determined to stick to my diet. Tomorrow I'd find that Richard Simmons exercise tape and sweat to the oldies.

#

At eight forty-five, on the nose, Sara, driving her dad's Chrysler, pulled into the drive. I left my station at the foyer window and hurried to the car. Sara turned as I climbed into the back seat and a gasp flew from my mouth. Her face was smeared in black. I put my hand to my heart. "You scared the crap out of me. What is this? Halloween?"

In answer, Sara held a flashlight under her chin in campfire horror story fashion. "Whooooo," she said, with a wavering eerie voice.

Karen's face was darkened too. She tossed a hockey puck shaped can of shoe polish at me. "You should put some on Margaret. We can't be too careful."

Sara backed out of the drive. "I can see it in the headlines now. 'PTA Secretary Arrested.' I want to save Hazel if she's in danger, but I'm

37

scared."

I patted her shoulder and spoke to Karen. "I know this was my stupid idea, but have you worked out any details to this plan? Even if Albert shows up there's nothing strange about a man checking on his elderly stepmother, especially when she's been sick."

"I'm going to catch him in the act," Karen said.

"Like watch through the window?" Sara asked.

"Yes."

Sara slowed the car and braked at a stop sign. "What if someone sees us? They'll think we're Peeping Toms or burglars and call the police."

"We're not going to be arrested," Karen said.

"It's not impossible," Sara muttered as she cruised through the intersection.

An idea came to me. "What about this?" I offered. "Hazel's house is on the edge of town and her backyard butts up against the Houser's cornfield. If we park on the side street and cut through the cornfield to get to her backyard, no one will see us."

"That's good," Sara said.

Karen nodded her agreement. "And think about this," she said. "When we were kids, my brothers and I used to sneak into the town swimming pool after hours."

"Why doesn't that surprise me?" I said.

Karen flipped me the bird and went on with her story. "We had this rule. If the cops came we'd each run in a different direction. By the time he decided which of us to go after, we had a head start. He never did catch us."

"You've got to be kidding," I said. "First of all, you were kids and the cop was probably overweight and middle-aged — of course he couldn't catch you. Now we're the ones who are overweight and middle-aged."

"I beg your pardon," Sara said. "I'm only twenty-eight."

We were just a block from our destination. Anticipation of adventure zapped through the car. I felt like I were on the diet pills my dad used to give me. They're outlawed now, but illegal users call it speed. "Turn the headlights off, Sara," I said.

Karen reminded us. "Scattering is still our best chance if we're nabbed.

I sighed. "Okay, but I'm not putting this shoe polish on my face. I'm the one most likely to be caught. If my face is clean I can say I'm jogging."

The girls laughed and fear vanished. At this point I doubt even Sara would have turned back.

"Jogging?" Karen asked. "On a hot summer night? In a hooded sweatshirt?"

"Well, what are they going to do?" I asked. "Call me a liar? I've never even had a parking ticket. They might suspect differently, but I'd like to see them prove it."

Sara parked the car and turned to me. "Your house is closest, Margaret. If we have to scatter, we'll meet up at your place."

#

De-tasseling corn as teenagers had taught us to protect our arms from corn leaf cuts, so before we entered the cornfield, Karen and Sara paused to button down the sleeves of their dark-colored shirts. I looked to the skies. The last swirls of orange and pink were fading. Once we were in the corn, no one would see us.

I pulled the hood of Harry's sweatshirt over my head for further invisibility. Now that we were out of the air-conditioned car I was sweltering in my heavy clothing.

I led the way. Silently, single file, we crept through the narrow aisle between the lush towering rows of corn.

What in great heavens am I doing? I asked myself. *Sneaking around under the cover of corn stalks and the dark like a kid up to no good? People who subscribe to Modern Maturity magazine aren't supposed to be chasing after crazy men. Adventure for people my age is supposed to be a cruise to the Bahamas or a bus trip with the bank travel club.*

On the other hand, if Hazel's life was actually in danger I wanted to help. I felt a huge grin spreading over my face. I could scold myself, or use

Hazel as an excuse, but was I actually all that convinced Albert was trying to do her in?

Although … he was crazy.

Truth is, I was excited. I was having fun.

The corn was so thick it shut out any possibility of fresh air. We had to move sideways through the constricted strip between corn rows. I could feel sweat collecting in every crevice of my body. It ran from my forehead and burned my eyes, and when I tried to wipe it away with the back of my hand, my hand was so damp all I did was rub more salt in my eyes.

Karen swore in a stage whisper. "Damn it, Margaret. Quit flipping the leaves in my face."

"Don't follow so close and they won't hit your face," I answered.

Sara's voice was plaintive. "I can't breathe in here."

I assured her we were nearly there and we moved on through corn plants so healthy and green they didn't even rustle as we passed between the stalks.

When we reached Hazel's backyard, we crept behind her garage to watch for Albert. The three of us, shrouded in black, sat on the ground using the rear of the garage as a back-rest. There was a dim fingernail moon rising over the cornfield; stars popped out one by one to dazzle against a dark sky. I've always said we have more, and brighter, stars in Alta Grove than anyplace else.

At least it seems that way because they
don't have to compete with ubiquitous
city lights.

Sara reached into her shirt pocket
and pulled out a pack of gum.
Simultaneously, Karen and I stretched
out a hand and Sara filled them with
pieces of spearmint.

"Do you think he'll really come?"
Sara asked.

"He's already out of the house to
go to his meeting, so it makes sense
he'll stop," Karen said.

Sara hugged her shoulders. "I hope
he doesn't and we can just go home.
Window peeking is for sex perverts, not
relatively normal women."

Karen snapped her gum, leaned
forward, and speaking softly said, "You
know what all that corn makes me think
about?"

"A steam room?" I offered.

"No. Sweet corn on the cob with
real butter."

Sara smothered a giggle. "With
BLT's made from ripe tomatoes, still
warm from my garden."

"And at least four pieces of
bacon," I added.

"At *least* four," Karen said. "My
second mother in law was a squeeze.
She'd break two slices in half to make a
sandwich. And the tomato was sliced so
thin; all I could taste was bread." She
snapped her gum to show her disdain.

Then we heard a vehicle turn into
Hazel's drive.

#

I held an index finger to my lips
and crept to the edge of the garage. It
was Albert's green pickup. After a
moment the engine went quiet and Albert
emerged from the driver's seat. Three
sets of eyes watched from the safety of
the garage as he pulled a set of keys
from his pants pocket and let himself
into his stepmother's side door.

We waited for Albert to clear the
entry, then scrambled to the kitchen
window to keep an eye on the
refrigerator. Karen got there first but
wasn't anywhere near tall enough to see
inside.

Silently, Sara and I searched the
backyard for something she could stand
on, but there was nothing in sight.
Sara slipped into the garage.

I could see the beam of her
flashlight darting about through the
garage window. Every noise magnified in
the night stillness. My skin was
prickly with nerves and wet with
perspiration under Harry's sweatshirt.
The garage door creaked. I held my
breath until Sara came out with a
decrepit wooden ladder. "Here you go,
Margaret."

"There is no way I'm climbing that
thing," I whispered.

"I don't think it will hold me,"
Sara said.

Karen stepped forward. "I'll do
it. He's my creepy brother-in-law."

Karen carefully placed the ladder

43

under the window. Sara and I stationed
ourselves on each side of the ladder to
keep it steady. At the third rung Karen
was high enough to peek into the kitchen
and I relaxed a little.

A light went on in the back room of
the place next door, and we flattened
ourselves against the house. I expected
the door to fly open and Hazel's
neighbor to come out with a shotgun in
his hands, but after a moment the light
went out and all was silent.

Karen looked down from her perch.
"He's in the kitchen," she said in a
stage whisper. "Do you have the camera,
Margaret?"

I nodded, but when I took my hand
off the ladder to take the camera from
my sweatshirt pocket, the ladder swayed.

"What are you doing?" Karen asked,
sounding frazzled. "Don't let go. I
want to go higher."

I could feel the thump of my heart
as Karen stepped to the next rung.

"I've got the perfect view," she
said. "He's at the refrigerator now.
Give me the camera." As Karen leaned
down to take the camera from my hand,
there was a night-piercing crack. The
rung she stood on gave way. The ladder
smacked solidly against the house and
Karen hit the ground. Sara and I tried
to help her but Karen was already
getting to her feet.

"Scatter," I called.

I didn't look back. I took off
through the backyards. When I reached a

44

fence that blocked my path I cut through a side yard and crossed the street. After working my way through a maze of houses and yards for several blocks, I finally felt safe and took to the sidewalk.

#

It was several minutes before my heart quit pounding in my head. I pulled the sweatshirt off. A breeze licked at the wet skin on my back, sending a cooling chill down my spine. It felt good. When my breathing normalized I told myself, *I'm just a woman taking a late evening stroll.* But inside I was exhilarated, pleased with myself. I felt like a spy for the CIA.

It was going on ten and lights were on in most of the houses. When you drive you're watching the road, passing houses too quickly to notice, but walking gave me glimpses of window vignettes: a couple sitting on a sofa with the soft light of their television flashing across their faces, a man passing through his living room, a woman watering the plants in her kitchen window sill.

In the next block I noticed a car parked in the street, a Lexis, the same color as the Lexis Cindy Waveland sometimes drove. Kitty Samuels lived a half block south. I wondered if Grant was paying a visit to his mistress.

He could have parked there for the same reason we'd parked on the side street. Maybe Grant didn't want Kitty's

neighbors to catch on. I patted my
sweatshirt pocket to see if I still had
the camera. It was there. I paused
under the streetlamp to set the camera
for zoom lens and night shots, then
crossed the street and headed south.

Kitty's brick bungalow sat on a
large lot and was nearly hidden behind a
shoulder-high hedge fence. The front
was dark, but I could see a light
glowing deep inside the house. Grant
wouldn't risk the chance of being seen
by neighbors. He'd probably come and go
by the back door.

My best bet was to find a place to
hide in the backyard. In my mind I was
imagining Grant and Kitty clinging to
one another, kissing goodnight on the
back stoop. When I snapped the picture
they'd be so caught up in the passion of
the kiss they wouldn't even notice the
flash. I'd be a hero and my photo would
squash Grant's evil attempt to get
custody of Angie.

I was so caught up in the scenario I
wasn't watching where I walked. I
tripped over something and fell on my
face. I stayed put long enough to do a
mental checklist of body parts, and
everything seemed to be working.
Whatever I tripped over was big enough
and soft enough to break my fall. I got
to my feet.

There was something wet on my
hands.

I let my eyes adjust to the
shadows, and then looked down to see

what I'd fallen over. A squeaky gasp
escaped. Grant Waveland was lying on
his back with a knife in his throat,
eyes staring blankly at the starry
skies. I turned my hands up close to my
face.

Blood.

CHAPTER FOUR

I lost my virginity to Ryan Harrison in the hay mow of his family's barn the autumn after I turned sixteen. He was two years older and it broke my heart when he went off to college. We continued the relationship for a while but we were too young and too horny to sustain the bond for the duration of our college years.

I started seeing Harry, and Ryan met someone new, and that was that. But we'd had some unforgettable moments. When I close my eyes I can still feel the wonder of the first time I felt his bare skin against mine. Makes me weak in the knees.

Ryan came home after he graduated, took a job on the police force, and through the years worked his way up to Chief of Police. About ten years ago he was elected County Sheriff, a job he still holds. He married but it didn't last. Since then he's been linked with a lot of women, but he's never remarried.

Ryan had dark brown wavy hair, but

now that he's older, his sideburns are more silver than brown, and there are a few silver strands in that curl that always flops down on his forehead when he's due for a haircut.

He must work out. No man in his fifties could possibly look as good as Ryan unless he worked at it.

Ryan raked his hand through his hair to get the curl off his forehead, and took in the three of us, all lined up in my white plastic porch chairs. Karen and Sarah had washed the shoe polish from their faces, but we were still dressed head to toe in black.

He addressed the first question to me. "When you called you didn't mention anyone being with you when you found Grant Waveland's body. Were the three of you together?"

The porch light wasn't on. We were illuminated by the corner streetlight and a couple of citronella lanterns. I was glad Ryan couldn't see my face clearly, because I meant to be evasive. I'd stick to the truth as closely as possible without mentioning window peeking at Hazel's. "No. I was alone."

"Where were Sara and Karen?"

"Here on the porch waiting for me."

The corners of Ryan's mouth twitched but he held back the smile. "So, they came to visit and you left them on the porch to take a walk?"

"No, we all took a walk, but I'm slower so I told them to go ahead."

Ryan narrowed his eyes, not quite

believing my statement. He looked at Karen. "Is that what happened?"

"We're all trying to lose some weight so we walk for exercise," Karen said. "Margaret's older and she doesn't like to hold us back. We went ahead and agreed to meet up here … on the porch."

Ryan still wasn't convinced. He watched my face and asked, "Don't you think it's dangerous? Walking at night? Dressed in black?"

"Black is slimming," I said.

The best defense is a good offense. That's what Harry always told me. I went on the attack. "What we're wearing has nothing to do with the fact that Grant Waveland is lying dead in Kitty Samuels' side yard."

"That's another thing," Ryan said. "I checked. Kitty has a tall row of bushes across the front of her property. You couldn't have seen Grant's body from the street. What were you doing in her yard?"

My mind was spinning, trying to come up with a feasible answer. "I, err…." I looked at the other girls apologetically. "I cheated. I was too tired to do the whole route so I started cutting through yards on the way home. That's how I found Grant. I tripped over the body."

Now I was the damsel in distress. "It was horrible. I got his blood all over my hands when I fell on him." I stared down at my hands like Lady Macbeth, then looked up at Ryan to see if he was swallowing the performance.

He wasn't.

He crossed his arms over his chest. "On this walk you took … did any of you happen to cut through Hazel Minnert's back yard?"

Sara gasped and looked at me wide-eyed. I shot her a look that said I'd smack her if she said a word.

"Why no, Ryan," I said.

"Did something happen at Hazel's?" Karen asked, with wide-eyed innocence.

Ryan kept his attention on Sara. "Her son, Albert, reported a window peeper."

Sara sat frozen, her green eyes wild and her lip aquiver. I knew she was imagining those headlines in next week's Alta Grove Messenger, 'PTA Secretary Arrested.'

I spoke to Ryan. "She wasn't anywhere near Kitty's house and she didn't see the body or anything else that concerns Grant's death."

Ryan's eyes held mine for a few seconds. It's possible he harbors a few fond memories of me too, because he dropped the Hazel thing. "I need to get back to the crime scene," he said. He tipped his cap and looked at me through narrowed eyes. "I'll be talking to you tomorrow, Maggie."

#

Murder in Alta Grove was incomprehensible. I was two years old the last time it happened. Amos Myer killed his wife with an axe and the event grew to legendary proportions.

The Myer farm house stood empty for decades, and as teenagers we'd drive out there and dare one another to walk the long dirt driveway from the road to the Myer house. I got up the nerve just once.

A canopy of sugar maples blocked the moon and stars. I bravely walked the overgrown trail, my flashlight beam darting about, casting pale circles of illumination as I searched the brush for zombies or some other version of the undead.

When I reached the decaying shell of the Myer house, the wind stirred a hanging screen door. I could see, in my mind's eye, old man Myer stepping out that door. I tore off down the path as though he were two steps behind, swinging his axe.

Scaring the crap out of yourself at the Myer farm was an Alta Grove rite of passage. When they finally tore the house down we all felt a twinge of regret.

In small towns your family reputation can make or break you. You could be the smartest, most law-abiding person for miles around, but if you have the bad luck to be born into the Myer family, everyone assumes all that bad blood will eventually catch up with you.

The opposite is true if you're a Waveland. When one of their teenagers gets into trouble, it's just growing pains. Waveland's are all trusted to grow up to be pillars of the community.

Grant's murder set the town on its ear. My phone rang constantly when word got out I'd found the body. Everyone wanted the scoop. I finally pulled the plug on the phone so I could get something done.

I straightened the kitchen and was getting ready to jump in the shower, so I could get dressed, when the back door bell rang. I wanted to ignore it but the garage door was open so everyone could see I was home.

The bell rang again.

Grumbling under my breath I went to answer. John Gildenbond was standing there with a covered plate.

"Good morning, Ms.O'Brian." He looked me over with a disapproving frown. "Don't you ever get dressed?"

"John, we've been neighbors for several months. Do you think you could call me Margaret?"

"With your permission, I'll be happy to call you Margaret. I baked scones last night and thought you might like some with your morning coffee."

"Are you sick?"

"Of course not. Why would you ask?"

"Oh. I get it. You want to know all about my finding Grant's body."

John actually smiled. "I did hear the news at the post office this morning, and I admit to a degree of curiosity. It's not every day that your neighbor's involved in a murder investigation."

I was in no mood to go through another round of telling my story, and John read my body language perfectly.

"Let's start over," he said. "Last night, while I was baking, I had second thoughts about my overreaction to Ruby's little garden gift. That's when I decided to bring you scones." He handed me the plate. "I hope you enjoy the treat, Margaret."

Now I was the one having second thoughts. "I'm sorry, John. I'm a little edgy this morning."

He nodded, accepting my explanation. "I understand."

I was feeling like a nasty ten year old, until he added, "I'll leave you now, Margaret, so you can dress for the day."

#

To hell with the shower, I had more important things to attend to. Diet or no diet, there was no way I was going to toss homemade scones, I don't care how many calories they are.

Especially these.

I could see a generous scattering of cranberries and white chocolate chips peeking out from the surface of the delicacies, and I meant to indulge.

I poured a cup of English Breakfast tea and sat at the kitchen table with the unexpected treat. The first bite crumbled in my mouth and the surge of endorphins was heavenly. It would take an hour of hell on the treadmill to wipe

out these five minutes of heaven, but I
didn't care.

#

As I was clearing crumbs from the
table, the doorbell rang again. This
time it was the front door. "Rats," I
said aloud. "This place is Grand
Central." I peeked out the window.
Ryan's official sheriff's car was in the
drive.

It's not that I had any particular
designs on Ryan. I don't regret
marrying Harry and I've no intention of
ever marrying again. It's just that
Ryan was my first love and I'd like him
to be secretly languishing away for me,
sorry he'd let me slip through his
fingers.

As if it weren't bad enough he'd
seen me in that getup the night before,
now I could blind him with my bright
orange PJ's with gaudy yellow
sunflowers. The cherry red toenail
polish was pretty special too.

I sighed and opened the door.
Ryan took in the garish pajamas,
and then grinned.

"Come in, Ryan."

He followed me to the kitchen and
took a seat at the table while I made a
pot of coffee. I wasn't sure what I was
feeling. Having Ryan in my kitchen was
disconcerting. Even though I was
innocent — innocent of murder anyway —
being questioned by the law made me feel
guilty.

I needed to quiet myself.

Performers say to picture the audience naked and it calms stage fright. As soon as that thought rolled into my mind, a flash of Ryan and me naked, rolling around on the creek bank when we were supposed to be fishing, popped into my head and I nearly dropped the pot of water I was pouring into the machine.

"Are you all right?" Ryan asked.

I turned to face him. Had he sensed my thoughts?

"Maggie, stumbling over a body had to be terrible for you."

Grant's body? Of course that was what he was talking about, and yes, it was terrible for me, but not as bad as it'd been for Grant. "I'm fine," I said. "Do I seem upset?"

"Not really, but that doesn't mean much. I remember when we were kids, you didn't like to talk about things that were bothering you."

"Then how did you know?"

Ryan's eyes crinkled as he grinned. "Your appetite would kick in and you'd crave salt."

The coffee pot was sizzling and chugging, so I hid my amazement by searching the cupboard for a cup and spoon. Last night I'd had a huge yen for potato chips. I'd nearly rolled out of bed at midnight to make a run to Quick Trip for a bag of Ruffles with Ridges.

Ryan and I hadn't done more than exchange pleasantries in over thirty years, yet he could still throw out this intimate detail of my personality.

"I need to ask a few questions about last night," Ryan said. "Like, what were you doing in Kitty's yard?"

I hesitated. *Should I plead the fifth?* Again Ryan saw through me.

"I don't care what you were doing at Hazel Minnert's. Actually that's not quite true, I would like to know why three women, of good reputation, were peeking in Hazel's window; however, I'm willing to let that go if you tell me why you were in Kitty Samuel's yard."

I blew out a breath of exasperation. Ryan was never going to let this go. I'd have to tell him. "I was trying to find out if Kitty and Grant were having an affair."

"And you wanted to know because?"

"Because, I like Grant's wife. You see … they've been having a few problems, and Cindy thought maybe Kitty was chasing after Grant, and they got into it, and Grant threatened to take custody of Angie if they divorced." I was running at the mouth faster than my head could consider the words. "Cindy thought he could get it done because she'd had a nasty bout of post-partum blues, and because he's such a hot shot lawyer…." I took a breath.

"Got it, Ryan said, but why were you in Kitty's yard?"

"Because, when I was … umm … out for a walk," I saw the Waveland's Lexus and knew Kitty lived right up the block. I had my camera and thought if I could

get a picture of Grant and Kitty kissing
or something, Cindy could use it for
leverage."

"You mean blackmail."

"Not exactly." I poured his
coffee, sat the remaining scone in front
of him, and sat down. "You know how
stuffy the Waveland's are. Grant
certainly wouldn't want his reputation
sullied and a picture like that would be
just the thing to get him to see reason
about custody of Angie if they actually
did get a divorce."

Ryan leaned toward me.
"Blackmail."

I leaned in too. "Semantics."

We each held our position for a
moment, then Ryan cracked. He sat back
in his chair and grinned at me. "You
haven't changed a bit. You're still a
wild woman."

Is he flirting with me?

"What made you take your camera
along on your late evening walk?"

"You never know when you'll see an
owl, or a new planet in the sky," I said
breezily.

Ryan shook his head in wonder.
"Where do you come up with this stuff?"

"More coffee?" I asked. Why did
having Ryan in my kitchen feel as though
the past thirty years were just thirty
minutes ago?

Ryan shook his head. His mug was
still more than half full. "This is
plenty. He took a bite of the scone,
sat back, and let the flavors meld.

"This is great," he said.

"Thanks," I said. No need for him to know I didn't bake.

Ryan's face became thoughtful. "Seems like Cindy had plenty of reason to be angry with her husband."

I could have smacked myself for having such loose lips when I realized I'd given Cindy motive for murder. I tried to back off. "I wouldn't say that. She was more sad than angry."

"She wasn't angry over his threat to take Angie?"

"Not really. She just seemed worried and sad."

Ryan leaned toward me. "You do realize most murder victims are killed by someone close to them?"

"That doesn't mean it had to be Cindy. She was crazy about Grant. She was fighting to keep him. Besides, if your hypothesis is right, Kitty Samuels would be just as suspect. Maybe Grant was trying to break it off because Cindy was on to them. If I was Kitty and some guy was rejecting me for the second time, I might be in the mood to do him in."

Ryan didn't seemed swayed by my argument. "Kitty may have had motive, but she also has an alibi," he countered.

"Where was she?"

"In Marshalltown at her parent's house."

Skepticism coated my words. "And you believe that? Of course her parents would vouch for her. Besides, if the killer was someone other than Kitty, why didn't the neighbors see anything?"

"For the same reason no one saw you in Kitty's yard. Those hedges were planted for privacy and they're doing the job."

Trepidation washed over me. I had to get Cindy off the hook. "Cindy's not very big," I said. "I don't see how she could have stabbed Grant."

"You'd be surprised at what people can do when the adrenalin's flowing, and it's not like Grant would've been expecting his wife to jump out of the bushes to stab him. She took him by surprise."

"I don't believe it. Besides, Cindy would never leave her kids alone, and I'm sure she didn't hire a babysitter so she could kill Grant." I raised my voice an octave. *There's coke in the refrigerator, dear. Help yourself. I won't be late. I'm just going out to kill my husband.*"

Ryan got to his feet, placed his hands on the kitchen table, leaned down and looked me straight in the eye. "She didn't have to get a babysitter. Mrs. Waveland says Cindy asked her to keep the kids for an overnight."

I was stunned. My mouth made gulping fish movements but nothing came out.

CHAPTER FIVE

Two hundred and six pounds.

I was down another pound despite the scone I'd eaten the day before. *That leaves me four more days*, I thought. If I'm good I can lose another pound before the next Fit Girl meeting.

The Fit Girl rule is to weigh yourself just once a week on Wednesday morning, but I can't help myself. I weigh nearly every morning. At least I've broken the habit of getting on the scale three times a day. Talk about obsessive.

I actually got out of my pajamas by nine. Karen and Sara were on their way over. Normally we'd meet at the coffee shop, but I was attracting attention everywhere I went because of finding Grant's body, so I wanted to lay low for a few days.

I made coffee for the girls and put a bag of English Breakfast tea in a cup of water to microwave for me.

They arrived together. Karen was holding an open house in the afternoon so she was dressed in one of her no-

nonsense work outfits, a solid tan
pencil skirt, with white-capped sleeve
blouse worn outside the skirt and belted
at the waist, and simple gold jewelry.

Sara wore Capri pants, in navy, to
make her ample butt appear smaller, and
a bright floral top meant to draw
attention to the smaller top half of her
body. It worked. Besides, Sara's face
is so beautiful it's hard to focus on
anything else.

We took our cups to the dining room
table. The dining room furnishings suit
my old house. The table and chairs were
once my mother's. The china cabinet and
buffet came through Harry's family.
Hanging over the china cabinet is an
oval frame, with convex glass, that
protects a hand-painted photo of Harry's
handsome grandfather in his twentieth
year.

When we were first married, we were
able to buy a house, but weren't flush
enough for furniture. Our families
scrounged around for no longer needed
items to get us started.

As we were able, we replaced some
things with new, but I'd grown attached
to many of the older pieces, and to the
history of the people who'd donated
them. If I had a million dollars I'd
keep my dining room just as it is.

I seated myself at the table as
Sara was saying, "My youngest sister
called from Texas last night. She'd
already heard about Grant's murder. She
said nothing ever happens in Alta Grove

until she leaves town."

None of us were surprised to hear how quickly the news had traveled.

"Did you tell her about our stakeout?" Karen asked.

"Yes, and she couldn't believe the sheriff knew it was us."

"Just play dumb," I said. "Ryan might have a good idea we were the peepers, but he can't do a thing about it unless one of us talks. With Grant's murder to deal with he doesn't have time for the small stuff."

"Besides, Sara, it's your fault," Karen said. "You gave me a piece of gum and we all know I can't walk and chew gum at the same time. Let alone climb a ladder."

That momentarily brought a smile to Sara's face. The smile dissipated when she had another thought. "I hate it that we scared Hazel," she said.

Karen stood and paced the room. "Jean Ann said Hazel was sick yesterday. I don't think it's a coincidence that Albert was at her house Wednesday night and on Thursday Hazel gets sick. And I did see him messing in the refrigerator"

"I'm not going back there," Sara said.

"Relax, Sara. You don't have to go back," I said. "And Karen, sit down, you're making me nervous with all that pacing."

Karen sat. "I wonder what he puts in the food."

"If anything, my guess would be

arsenic," I mused. "It's the easiest to get a hold of. Every farmer in the area has an old box of rat poison on the farm."

Karen was on her feet pacing again. "That slime ball."

"I have an idea," I announced.

Sara stuck her lower lip out and blew out air. "Do I even want to hear this? The last time you had an idea I ended up scaring a sweet old lady."

Karen held her hand out to hush her. "I want to hear it. Go on, Margaret."

"What if we stake-out Hazel's place again, but this time we stay in the car until Albert shows. After he leaves we pay Hazel a social call. One of us will stay with the car as lookout. One of us can keep Hazel busy while the other gets samples of food from the leftover containers in her refrigerator."

Karen's shoulders perked up. "That could work. We could have the food tested for arsenic, and Albert's fingerprints would be all over the plastic bowls."

"Right," I said. "If they find anything in the food we tell Ryan and he can take it from there."

Sara set her coffee aside. "Why can't we just tell him what we suspect now?"

Karen sighed and explained carefully. "Because Jean Ann would never speak to me again if I'm wrong about this."

Sara nodded. "Got it."

"Do you think you could get your dad's car for us?" Karen asked.

Sara reluctantly agreed. "Okay, I'll get dad's car, and I'll even be the getaway driver. But I'm not getting out of the car, and if Albert or the police come while you two are inside, I'll lay on the horn, but then I'm leaving you."

#

That afternoon, since I was dressed, I decided to return John Gildenbond's plate. As anal as he is, he was probably getting nervous over his missing china.

He answered the door bell promptly. "The scones were fantastic," I said, as I offered the plate.

"Come in." He opened the screen door wide.

I hadn't expected to be invited inside, but then I hadn't expected homemade scones either.

I sat at Gildenbond's cozy table and looked around the kitchen as he poured sun tea over a glass of crystal ice. The table was covered with a yellow floral cloth that matched the ruffled curtains at the windows, and the house smelled of fresh-baked brownies.

The ice tinkled as John set the tea in front of me and then placed a cloth napkin alongside the glass.

"You're full of surprises," I said.
"How so?"
"For one, this room, it's so welcoming, and you're obviously

comfortable in a kitchen."

"Yes, I've always enjoyed cooking, and now that I'm retired I'm trying my hand at baking."

"What did you do for a living?"

"Taxes. I'm a CPA."

Somehow he seemed better suited to work as a revenue collector for the government. I asked the question all we lifers ask people who move here. "What brought you to Alta Grove?"

"San Francisco's an expensive city to live in when you're retired. I was born and raised in Iowa so it was a natural place to consider when I decided to leave."

"Do you miss the city?"

"Not really."

He dabbed his lips with his napkin and I was struck by how kissable they were. I don't mean I wanted to kiss the man. He was too fastidious for my taste. But his lips were full and I bet he'd never smoked a cigarette in his life, because the space above his upper lip was wrinkle free.

That's one of my biggest regrets about smoking for twenty some years. It's been six years since I lit my last Winston and the smoking wrinkles over my lip are as deep as ever. It'd take plastic surgery to be rid of them.

"I suppose murder was an everyday occurrence in San Francisco," I said.

John considered for a moment. "Yes, but its different here. Everything in Alta Grove is personal.

In San Francisco I never met my
neighbors. In the few short months I've
been here, everyone on Ascension Street
has introduced themselves. Merle Jansen
even invited me to join his men's golf
league."

I felt proud of my town's
friendliness and it seemed to be rubbing
off on John. I hoped so. I wouldn't
mind an occasional delivery of scones.

John continued. "In San Francisco
a killer would be faceless, in Alta
Grove the killer could be someone I
know." He cocked his head and raised an
eyebrow. "Perhaps even my eccentric
pajama-wearing neighbor. After all, you
discovered the body."

"I doubt I'd make a viable suspect.
I only knew Grant to say hello, although
his wife and I are friendly."

"He wasn't your lawyer?"

"No. He never struck me as a man I
wanted to know my business."

John raised his glass of tea in
salute to me. "I think you're a woman
who knows people."

Maybe John Gildenbond wasn't a bad
guy after you got to know him. If I
made sure Ruby didn't get loose and kept
the hedges between our properties
trimmed, maybe we could be friends.

#

I spent the rest of the day on
housework, catching up on laundry and
vacuuming cobwebs in the basement. My
hair was sticky with fine dusty threads.
Hauling the vacuum up and down the

stairs and dragging it around the
basement had been hard work. I felt good
about burning so many calories. After
my shower, since I was already naked, I
stepped on the scales.

Two hundred and seven pounds.

Up a pound since morning. That was
good. I usually weighed two pounds more
in the afternoon than in the morning, so
I was actually down a pound.

Two hundred and five was my true
weight.

Still in my birthday suit, I dashed
upstairs to find fresh pajamas. I chose
the pink polka-dot set I'd bought in the
Smoky Mountains. Some people buy a
spoon or a tee-shirt with the name of
the place they're visiting, I buy PJ's.

I like them a size too big and in
cotton, no see-through stuff. I don't
want to bother with a robe. I wear
pajamas like some people wear sweats. I
only put on real clothes when I'm
expecting guests or leaving the house.

For dinner I had a buffalo burger,
baked chips and salad. Buffalo's my
latest diet discovery. It tastes a lot
like beef, slightly sweeter, and has,
depending on the cut, seventy to ninety
percent less fat. It's also lower in
cholesterol and higher in protein. But
the best part is, three ounces of
buffalo is less than a hundred calories,
so I ate six ounces.

With my stomach satisfied, I opened
the laptop. Ruby likes to be near me
when I work on the computer. She sleeps

in a little box smack dab next to the machine. I spent some time reading and sending emails to the kids, and then I brought up my diet diary and listed the food and caloric count of each item.

I've read that dieters who keep a log of what they eat each day lose more weight. You're not supposed to wait until the end of the day to record the food because it's so easy to forget little bits and pieces you shove in your mouth.

They're right. I list everything I remember, add up the day's calories and think, *Wow, that was a pretty good day, only fifteen hundred calories.*

About the time I walk away from the computer I remember the mini Snickers I bought when I was paying the clerk at the drug store and I say to myself, *That was just two bites, I'll add fifty calories. Fifteen hundred and fifty is still a great day.*

Then the nuts I ate while I was playing cards with the bridge group will pop into my head. *Okay, add another two hundred. Seventeen fifty is still a decent day.* By the time I remember the banana I had in the middle of the night when I got up to pee, and add that eighty calories, the count isn't looking so sweet.

What I wanted to do next was settle into my book, and then later, an evening of television, but my conscience was pricking at me. Grant had been killed on Thursday night and I still hadn't contacted Cindy. It wasn't that we were that close. After she resigned from teaching, we'd got met for lunch a few times a year, and that was the extent of the friendship until she'd called to ask about Fit Girls.

Still, I liked Cindy, and her recent confidences about her marital problems, and the fact that I'd found Grant's body, tied me to her. I certainly didn't want to go over there. Maybe a phone call would do it.

Before I could follow through with the thought, the phone rang. It was Karen.

"I went for a walk with Jean Ann earlier. She said she's having a night out with a girlfriend, and Albert's going to Hazel's for dinner. He'll be leaving any time now. Let's roll."

#

Sara parked her dad's Chrysler a few houses down from Hazel's simple ranch style home. Hazel and Albert's father had moved to town when they retired from farming. Owning farm land in McCall County is like owning a gold mine. Hazel has the big bucks. She's a millionaire several times over, but wealthy people in Alta Grove seldom flaunt it.

"I don't know why we couldn't wait until Albert was out of here," Sara said.

Karen rolled her eyes. "Because if there's something in the food I want to be able to tell the sheriff we gathered

the leftovers from Hazel's dinner right
after Albert left. That way Albert
can't say someone else did it."

Sara sighed. "At least I didn't
have to put shoe polish on my face."

"There he is," I said. "Albert's
headed for his truck."

We all watched as Albert backed out
of Hazel's drive.

"Get down," Karen said.

We crouched in our seats as the
truck roared past, then one by one, Sara
last, we risked a peek to be sure he was
really gone.

Karen and I got out of the Chrysler
and I leaned into Sara's open window.
"Are you sure you don't want to come
in?"

"I'm sure. And don't be long. I
feel like my stomach's full of jumping
beans."

"Sara, it's still daylight.
Nothing's going to happen. We're just
paying a social call on Hazel. No big
deal."

"Tell that to the judge," she said.
#
Hazel was glad to see us and
invited us to sit in the living room.
Like a lot of older people she hadn't
kept up with the latest decorating
styles and colors. Big Henry and Little
Hank were hanging above the television.

Decades ago, the picture of the big
owl and a smaller owl sitting on a
branch had been the biggest seller for a
home interior company that sold their

wares by the party method. It'd been a while since I'd seen it, but for years half the homes in America had a version of that print on their wall.

"We've been wondering how you're doing," I said.

"I haven't been up to par, and I've lost weight, but today I'm better," Hazel answered. "Thank goodness for Albert. He checks on me all the time."

"That's great," I said, but I was thinking she didn't look good. The skin on her face sagged from the recent weight loss, and her voice reflected low energy.

Hazel sat and rearranged the doilies on the arm of her chair. "I never dreamed Albert would come around like he has. He resented it when I married his dad. I did my best, but he was a difficult boy." She turned to Karen. "When he married your sister I felt bad for her. But I was wrong about Albert. He's not always pleasant, but he has a good heart."

Hazel put a hand to her cheek. "I'm forgetting my manners. I have fresh lemonade. I'll get you some."

I got to my feet in a flash. "Please don't get up," I said. "Let me get it."

#

Hazel's kitchen was large with ample eating space. It was decorated '70s style with dark cupboards and yellow wallpaper printed with mushrooms and birds. The faint odor of cabbage hung in the air.

I put on a pair of skinny latex gloves, and then pulled the plastic grocery bag from my pants pocket. My head was deep into the refrigerator when I felt the tap on my shoulder. Startled, I jerked up, hit my head on the top of the appliance, and dropped the container of corned beef.

Karen's eyes were ready to pop. She grabbed a paper towel from the counter and dropped to her knees to clean the mess. "Didn't you hear the horn?" she asked.

The kitchen door opened and we froze, me with meat-stained gloves and plastic bag dangling from my wrist, Karen on her knees with corned beef splattered in front of her. Albert's mouth was open and he had an angry glare in his eyes.

"Is that you Albert?" Hazel called from the living room. "Did you get the milk?"

CHAPTER SIX

For several seconds the room was so quiet I could hear the clock on the wall ticking. Karen and I were transfixed. We waited for Albert's reaction to release us from the spell. He looked like the Jack and the Bean Stock giant standing in the door.

"What the hell are you doing here?" His voice was low, barely under control. If Hazel hadn't been in the next room it would have been worse.

I don't know where it came from, but I said, cool as a cucumber, "Hazel asked me to get everyone lemonade and I dropped the container of meat." Whatever else he was, Albert wasn't stupid.

"What's with the gloves, Margaret?" I just stood there with my mouth hanging open, but Karen stood up, tossed the meat and the container in my plastic bag and said, "Allergies. Margaret's hands are broken out from using a skin cream. She was allergic to something in it."

I'm sure Albert didn't swallow that

one either, but Hazel came in. "I'm so sorry, Hazel," I said, "I've made a mess."

Hazel patted my shoulder. "Accidents happen, dear. Don't worry. It'll save me from having to eat leftovers."

Karen finished cleaning the floor and put the paper towels in the trash. "Gotta go, Hazel. Margaret and I are playing bridge with the girls tonight." She wiggled her fingers at Albert, "See ya later, brother-in-law."

\#

Karen and I were halfway to my house by the time Sara picked us up. By then I was a sweat-ball and I still had the tang of corned beef and cabbage in my nostrils.

"Oh my god, Sara," I said, when we got in the car. "You should've seen Albert's face. He was steaming."

"I tried to warn you. I practically laid on the horn.

"I know," Karen said. "But Margaret made a mess in the kitchen and we couldn't get out fast enough."

"What did he say when he saw the two of you?"

"He wanted to know what in the hell we were up to," I answered.

"But … did you get the evidence?"

Karen held the plastic bag up so Sara could see. "The meat juices might have messed up any fingerprints on the container, but we have the corned beef. I'll have it tested for arsenic."

Sara held her shoulders tight, and then shivered. "I can't even remember the last time something bad happened in Alta Grove. Now Grant Waveland's been murdered and Albert may be poisoning poor Hazel."

"It's been three years," I said. "Three years ago Alice Crowley was caught embezzling money from the school. I hadn't retired yet. I'll never forget it. I had such a hard time believing Alice would do such a thing."

Karen stroked her lip in thought. "That was a shocker. I would never have believed Alice capable of theft if she hadn't pleaded guilty. I wonder what happened to her."

"I don't know," Sara said. "I haven't even thought about her in ages."

I thought of Alice often. She was a great reader and she and I had had a lot of interesting conversations about books. "She got permission from her parole officer to leave the state so she could live near her family," I said. "I would've done the same thing. It'd be impossible to live in Alta Grove with something like embezzlement hanging over your head."

#

At home I spent a half hour in the tub soaking the cabbage stink away, then went to my room for fresh pajamas. The air conditioning clicked on and a fresh burst of cold air rushed through my bedroom register. I quickly donned my blue PJ's with tuxedo cats chasing bright-colored balls of yarn.

Book in hand, I crawled into bed and tried to relax against a stack of pillows. The bath had taken the edge off but I was still wired. I tried reading, but the words weren't sinking in. My thoughts kept going back to Cindy Waveland.

It looked bad for her. She had both motive and opportunity, but I was convinced she was innocent. Kitty might have an alibi, but what she didn't have were scruples. There was a girl who was capable of murder, and there had to be a reason Grant's body was in her yard.

I set the book aside and shut off the lamp. Ruby jumped up on the bed and started kneading my thigh, a low purr rumbling in her throat. Eventually she snuggled against my leg.

The last thought that floated through my mind before sleep came was that, somehow, I had to convince Ryan to take another look at Kitty Samuels.

#

The couple that had lived previously in John Gildenbond's house, Michelle and Ron Haley, had been busy young people who worked in Waterloo. They'd leave for work by eight in the morning, leaving me with the privacy to water flowers or have breakfast on the porch in my pajamas.

I missed the Haley's and Ruby did too. They were cat lovers and had owned a huge Maine Coon they called Puddy. We would exchange pet sitting when we vacationed. Ruby was used to spending time at their house and the Haley's didn't mind when Ruby strolled over to visit. If they were still my neighbors I could have let Ruby come to the porch with me.

I'd just set my breakfast tray aside when John Gildenbond climbed the stairs. It was only eight but the temperature was quickly climbing and the air was full of moisture. It made me feel rumpled. John was, as usual, impeccable: shorts sharply creased, and that beautiful white hair full of healthy clean shine.

"Good Morning, Margaret.

John took in the PJ's but didn't comment. Was he going to show up every time I breakfasted on the porch?

He took the white plastic chair next to mine. "I saw the obituary for that Waveland guy in the Waterloo paper," he said. "The article said he served on the hospital board and he was also the Rotary club's president. Sounds like he was a pretty important man in this area. No wonder his death has caused such a stir."

"Grant had his fingers in a lot of pies," I said.

"Have you learned anything new about the murder?"

I hadn't yet decided how friendly I wanted to be with Gildenbond. He was growing on me, but the idea of some lonesome man hanging around all the time didn't fit into my life plan.

Well, the truth was: I no longer had a life plan. I thought Harry and I would grow old and cantankerous together, kind of like Diana and Tom on that British sitcom, *Waiting for God*. Guess I needed a new plan, Stan.

"You probably know more than I do," I said. "I've been staying close to home."

"By virtue of being the neighbor of the woman who discovered the body, I was the most popular guy on the golf course yesterday. Everyone thinks I have inside information."

I could have given John a few gory details, told him about the blood on my hands, or how Grant's vacant eyes had stared up at the stars, but I didn't have the heart to talk about it. Not that I can't dish the dirt with the best of them, but thoughts of Cindy and the turmoil in her life were zipped in my lips.

John realized he'd hit the wrong note. "I'm sorry if I offended you, Margaret. I really don't care about the local gossip. I was . . . well, I enjoy your company and I was trying to make conversation. I guess I was clumsy about trying to get to know you better."

Maybe my pajamas were more alluring than I realized. "I'm not offended," I said. "It's just that Grant's wife is a friend of mine so I'm not comfortable about second-guessing the situation. And truly, I haven't heard anything since I found Grant's body."

The sheriff's car pulled into the drive. *Must be my morning for gentlemen callers.*

Ryan stepped out of the car. It was Sunday so he was out of uniform for a change. I watched as he approached the porch, appreciating the way he looked in his jeans and tee-shirt.

"Good morning, Maggie."

Maggie.

Ryan is the only one who still uses my old school nick name. I liked it. "Good Morning, Ryan. Have you met my neighbor?"

John stood and offered his hand. "John Gildenbond," he said. I'm renting the house next door."

Ryan was a half head taller. His body had long lean muscles, like a runner. John's is a weightlifter's bulkier build. His legs were tan from time spent on the golf course. I couldn't ever remember seeing Ryan in a pair of shorts. He probably had a farmer's tan, brown face and arms and snow white torso and legs.

"Good to meet you," Ryan said. "I'm sorry to interrupt but I have a few things to discuss with Maggie. Could you give us a few minutes?"

"Of course." John turned to me. "I'm making BLT's and sweet corn for lunch. Will you come?"

"BLT's? I'll be there."

John nodded. "Noon then."

#

Ryan took John's place in the

80

plastic chair, stretched his legs out in front and folded his arms over his chest. All he needed was a cowboy hat and a piece of grass to stick in his mouth.

"Getting pretty friendly with the new neighbor," he said.

I bit back a smile. "Not really. I haven't decided how I feel about him."

"You're having lunch with him. Sounds pretty friendly to me."

"I'd have lunch with the devil if he were serving BLT's with tomatoes fresh from the garden."

"He hasn't lived here long enough to put a garden in."

"Maybe not, but Sara keeps me well supplied with tomatoes and I'll take some over when I go."

He looked me over, his eyes narrowing in disapproval. "Do you think you should be entertaining strange men on the porch in your pajamas? Some guys would get the wrong idea."

Between John's past comments, and now Ryan on his high-horse over my PJ's, I snapped. "If people would call before they come over I'd get dressed to entertain them. Otherwise they can take me like they find me and that's probably in my pajamas."

Ryan's eyes sparkled and I knew he was trying not to laugh. That made me madder. "If you have another word of advice about what I choose to wear, I'm going inside and locking the door."

Ryan put his hands up in surrender,

and managed to get his budding grin
under control. "You're right and it's
none of my business anyway. Got any
coffee?"

Mollified, I let the matter drop. I
answered stiffly. "I can make a pot, or
I have an instant coffee bag.

"Instant is good. I don't have a
lot of time."

#

Inside, I put his coffee mug in the
microwave. The trouble with constantly
being on a diet is there's seldom
anything good to serve to a guest. Ryan
would have to make do with coffee.

Once he was settled at the table
with his brew, Ryan was all business.
"When you were the school librarian,
what did you hear about Grant and Kitty
seeing one another?"

So, it wasn't a casual visit. Ryan
was working. I was glad to supply any
information that kept him from zeroing
in on Cindy. "It may not have gotten
out in the community at large," I told
him, "but in the school system we all
knew they were an item. She and Grant
were hot and heavy. Kitty's husband
left her because of it."

"Cindy was teaching at the time
wasn't she?"

Here we go with Cindy again, I
thought. "Yes, but she and Grant
weren't seeing one another yet. Cindy's
a beautiful woman. The year she moved
to Alta Grove to teach at the high
school she turned every male head in the

county."

Ryan grinned. "I remember."

"It wasn't long before she caught Grant's eye. He dropped Kitty like a hot potato."

"So Kitty lost out all round," Ryan said. "Her husband was gone and she didn't land Grant either. Think she's still angry?"

"I thought she had an alibi? Didn't you say Kitty was in Marshalltown with her family?"

"That's right, but it's my job to uncover everything I can about the people in Grant's life."

It dawned on me that Ryan might suspect Kitty's family was covering for her or . . . I spoke out loud as the thought came to me: "Kitty could have hired someone."

"It's possible."

"I'm glad you're taking a look at someone besides Cindy," I said. "I can't imagine her sticking a knife in Grant's neck. God knows why, but she still loved the man."

Ryan sat the coffee mug on the table and looked at me. "I know you're feeling guilty. You think I suspect Cindy of killing her husband because of what you told me, but cracks in people's relationships eventually reveal themselves in any investigation.

When I talked to Grant's mother the night he was killed, she told me her son's marriage had problems. In fact, that's why she took her granddaughter

that evening. She was hoping if Cindy
and Grant had time to talk without
distractions, they'd work things out.
So stop feeling guilty."

I released my hunched shoulders and
sat back in my chair, letting go of all
the tension caused by my imagined
culpability.

"Feel better?" Ryan asked.

I laughed. "Yes I do. But I still
want to know about Kitty. Where is
she?"

"She's staying in Marshalltown.
Said she wouldn't be able to sleep in
her house knowing Grant's body was found
in her yard."

My mind was awash with ideas.
"Maybe it's her guilty conscience that
keeps her away? Maybe Grant wasn't
having an affair with her, but Kitty was
trying to start something up again?
Maybe he turned her down and Kitty was
angry? Or maybe they *were* sleeping
together, and when Cindy confronted him,
Grant broke it off with Kitty for a
second time? That would be reason to
kill him."

Ryan listened, but didn't seem
affected by the flood of words. "That's
a lot of maybes," he said. "I think I'd
better go out and dig up some facts."
He finished off his coffee and stood.
"I've got to go Maggie." He paused, and
then said quietly, "I want you to stay
out of this."

My eyes opened wide. "What makes
you think I want to be mixed up with

murder?"

"Don't give me that innocent look.
I'm worried about that curious nature of
yours. You jump into things without
thinking it through."

I stood, ready to defend his
assessment of me, but Ryan reached out
to clasp my upper arms. His hands were
gentle, but the flint in his eyes told a
different story. For a nanosecond, I
thought he was going to shake me, but
instead he dropped his hands and took a
step back.

"There's a killer out there, Maggie.
I want you to take it seriously." He
ran a hand through his hair, sweeping
the stray curls from his forehead, then
he locked them in place by putting his
cap on with a back to front motion.

I walked Ryan to the door. With
his hand on the knob, he spoke again.
"No running around town dressed in black
to spy on anyone."

My face split into a grin.

"I'm not kidding, Maggie. I swear,
I'll arrest you if you pull any of your
shenanigans."

#

I now understood that I'd avoided
calling Cindy out of shame. I'd felt so
bad about spilling my guts to Ryan, I
couldn't face her. Now that Ryan had
eased my guilt, I was ready to make the
long-delayed call to Cindy. "Are you all
right?" I asked when she answered.

"As all right as I can be. It's so
strange. I still can't believe Grant's

SANDRA NOBLE

gone."

"I'm so sorry, Cindy."

"The sheriff's been here twice. Grant's parents had Angie the night he was killed so I don't have an alibi. I was here, alone, waiting for him to come home." Her voice shook with emotion. "They think I killed my husband."

"Are you alone, Cindy?

"My parents and sister are here. After the funeral tomorrow, Mom and Dad are taking Angie back to Minnesota with them. My sister's staying here for a while. She teaches in Minneapolis so she has the summer free."

It made me feel a lot better to know Cindy's family was being supportive.

"I keep thinking about the past few weeks," she said. "My worries about Kitty, that stupid argument about getting a divorce … it's like all the happy times we spent together don't mean a thing and the last two weeks define the whole marriage. The divorce threats I made haunt me. I still don't know what happened to us. If only our last week together had been different. I wish I could go back and make it right."

She seemed to be talking to herself as much as to me, and I could hear the tears in her voice as she continued.

"Grant's law practice is going strong. Our new house is beautiful. I was so pleased to be able to stay home with Angie. It was just what we'd planned. I should have been happy.

Instead I stuffed my face, gained weight and drove Grant away from me."

"Cindy, quit beating yourself up. Staying home with kids isn't the easy job husbands think it is."

Cindy sighed. "The highlight of my day was Grant coming home from work. But he kept coming home later and later all the time. I felt like I was losing him."

My heart was breaking for her. "You weren't losing him, Cindy. You were just experiencing the same adjustment period we all go through after the first baby comes. And I'm sure gaining a few pounds didn't keep Grant from loving you."

I could hear as Cindy blew her nose, hiccupped, and tried to pull herself together. "My biggest fear isn't being a murder suspect, it's that Grant didn't love me anymore — that he and Kitty laid in bed together, laughing at me for being a dull housewife whose biggest concern was diaper rash."

It was time to give the girl a dose of tough love. "First, you have no proof Grant and Kitty had anything going on other than business. And second, every marriage has its bad times. Do you think there weren't times I didn't dream of the double indemnity clause in Harry's insurance policy? That doesn't mean I didn't love him.

And as pissed as he could be with me, I always knew it was a temporary situation. You and Grant would have pulled it together."

Cindy sniffled. "I know you're right, Margaret. You always make me feel better. You will come to the funeral tomorrow, won't you?"

I hadn't planned on going to the funeral. I'd planned to get by with sending flowers, but Cindy was asking for my support. Heaven knows she needed all the comfort she could get. Losing a husband was bad enough, I ought to know, and to be the prime suspect in his murder was beyond imagining.

"Certainly," I said. "I'll see you tomorrow."

CHAPTER SEVEN

Sara couldn't be convinced, but I talked Karen into going to the funeral with me. The Catholic church, a stately gray stone building, with somber dark-toned stained glass windows, is just three blocks from my house, so we walked. Good thing because there wasn't any place to park. Cars overflowed the church parking lot and lined the streets.

Karen and I stood in line to sign the book, and then joined the procession of mourners walking the purple-carpeted aisle until we found a pew with room for two more bodies.

Mable and Tom Sterling, who owned the grocery store, nodded solemnly as we squeezed in beside them. I avoided conversation with them, because I was afraid Mable would eventually ask me about finding Grant's body. I pretended to be engrossed by the stained glass windows, and the statues at each station of the cross, and finally by turning my attention to the funeral handout.

As I read, I was increasingly

distracted by smatterings of soft conversations of people greeting one another and speaking in hushed whispers of the horror of murder in Alta Grove.

Claustrophobia played around my chest, a tap here, a nudge there. I wasn't sure if it was the crush of people, the sweet scent of Mable's floral perfume, or the fact that I just plain didn't want to be there, but I was finding it difficult to stay put. I looked around for a reason to stand. Maybe I could excuse myself to use the bathroom. A woman my age always has to pee. I checked my watch. If the service started on time, I had five minutes.

I was calculating the number of people I'd have to disturb to get to the aisle, when I saw an elderly couple pass our pew, searching for a place to sit. The woman was small and bent over her cane. The husband kept a careful eye on her but was having some balance problems himself. Perfect. I nudged Karen and motioned toward them, silently asking if we should offer our seats. Karen gave a nod of agreement.

The couple was grateful to take our places, and I was more grateful for the excuse to give them up. Karen and I went to the back of the church to wait as ushers brought folding chairs from the basement for the overflow.

Being free of Mable's perfume was like having holy water splashed in my face. I was revived. I scanned the crowd for familiar faces and did a double take when I saw something odd. At the very back, half hidden behind a pillar, stood a woman. She was tall and wore a shapeless navy blue dress that came to mid-calf, a hat with a wide brim, and big sunglasses. Her head was tilted down and I couldn't see the color of her hair because it was stuffed into the hat.

I gave Karen an elbow and spoke with my hand cupped to one side of my mouth. "Look toward the back of the church. The last pillar on your left."

Karen turned, assuming a nonchalant demeanor. When she spied the strange woman, she gave me a quizzical stare. "Rather mysterious, isn't she?" Karen said softly. "Is she trying to disguise herself?"

"That's what I was thinking. Can you make out who it is?"

Karen leaned toward me. "In that getup it might even be a man. I'll walk that way and get a better look."

Karen sauntered around for a few moments, quietly greeting friends, then walked past the mysterious figure.

"It is a woman," Karen said when she returned. "I could smell her shampoo, and no man has ankles that trim."

"She was a couple inches taller than you," I noted.

Karen agreed. "I'm wearing heels and her shoes were flat so I'd say she's at least five nine."

The clatter of metal folding chairs

quieted and people standing were taking
their seats so the service could start.

I touched Karen's arm. "Let's go."
In the confusion of people moving toward
the chairs we slipped through the crowd
unnoticed.

Karen's face was flush with
excitement as she followed me out the
door. "What are we doing?"

I hurried down the cement steps,
heels clicking. "We're going back to my
house to get the car. Our lady of
mystery doesn't want anyone to know who
she is, so she'll hang toward the back
of the church and be one of the first to
leave. We'll follow her home and see
who it is."

"I bet its Grant's killer," Karen
said. "The killer always goes to the
funeral."

CHAPTER EIGHT

Karen and I were in my Honda, ready
to return to the church, when I realized
I'd left my sunglasses on the kitchen
counter and went to retrieve them. When
I left the house for the second time, I
was in such a hurry I forgot to watch
for the kitty escape artist. Ruby
literately jumped at the opportunity and
flew down the porch steps.

We spent precious time trying to
find her before we gave it up. I could
only hope she'd stay out of John's
flowers.

#

The church parking lot took up half
a block and the church the other half.
I double-parked across from the parking
lot where we had a good view of the wide
front doors of the church.

The hearse was stationed at the side
door and the funeral procession would
line up behind it. I didn't worry about
the mysterious woman leaving from the
side to join the procession to the
cemetery. It was clear she didn't want
to be recognized so I didn't think she'd

want to be seen at the graveside service.

I was so intent on watching the church doors I forgot I was double-parked. I heard a car door shut, and in the side mirror saw Ryan walking toward us. "Rats."

Karen looked up to see what I was muttering about. "Here comes trouble," she said.

Ryan bent and leaned in the window. Suspicion glimmered in his deep blue eyes. "What are the two of you up to now?"

"Nothing," I said. "The church was crowded so we decided to wait and join the graveside service."

"You can't wait here. When the funeral's over this area will be congested with traffic."

There she was. The woman in black was coming down the church steps. "I'll move right now." I nudged Karen and nodded toward our mysterious lady.

Karen said, "You're right, Sheriff. We'll wait at the cemetery."

Ryan must have seen the look that passed between me and Karen. He held his place, his eyes searching mine.

"What are you up to, Maggie?"

I gave him my best baffled expression: mouth slightly open, eyes narrowed as if questioning his sanity. "Up to? I'm attending Grant's funeral. What do you think I'm up to?" Ryan may not have been fooled by my righteous indignation, but he stood back. I put

the Honda in drive and took off toward
the parking lot. I checked the rearview
mirror. "Ryan's still watching," I
said. "If I stop here he'll know
something's up. We'll have to turn
toward the cemetery."

"Now what?" Karen asked. "She'll
be long gone by the time we circle
around."

"I have a hunch about this. How
many women do you know who are five nine
or more in flat shoes?"

The light flashed in Karen's eyes.
"Kitty Samuels is that tall."

"Let's go straight to her place," I
said.

Karen agreed. "If we're wrong
we'll never know who the mysterious
woman is, but what choice do we have?"

"I don't think we're wrong," I
said.

Alta Grove has only two stoplights,
one block apart. As always, when you're
in a hurry, they were red when I
approached the heart of town. At least
they're timed to change simultaneously,
so I only had to stop once. I could only
hope the dark lady would be delayed by
traffic at the church ... and that the
dark lady was actually Kitty.

When we reached Kitty's
neighborhood, I parked a few houses down
and across the street from her house.
No sign of her yet. Maybe we were too
late, but I wanted to sit tight for a
while.

"All this tension's making me

hungry," Karen said. "Wish I had a candy bar and something to drink."

"We won't stay long. If Kitty doesn't show in a few minutes we've either missed her, or have this figured wrong."

Karen flipped the visor down and checked her makeup. "I'm never going on another stakeout without food."

I threw her a nasty glare. "Will you stop with the food. I'm trying to dump some poundage, you know. Just change the subject."

"Alright, but you won't like the new subject either."

"Anything's better than food."

Karen turned in her seat, waiting until I looked her full in the face. "What?" I asked.

"Are you sweet on the sheriff?"

My jaw dropped. "What are you talking about?"

"There's something there. I can feel the spark."

"You're crazy."

Karen put her chin in the air with stubborn defiance. "I am not crazy. When he was questioning us on the porch the night you found Grant's body, he kept watching you."

"He was just trying to figure out what was going on. I mean, think about it. It was ten o'clock at night and the three of us were dressed in black and lined up like those see-no-evil, hear-no-evil, speak-no-evil monkeys."

"Sara said her mother told her you

and Ryan Harrison were sweethearts when you were in high school."

Was nothing ever forgotten in a small town? "Ancient history," I said. "Besides, I don't tell you guys everything. For instance, I had lunch with John Gildenbond yesterday."

Karen's eyes widened. "You said John was a grumpy, persnickety, cat hater."

"I know, but it turns out he has a sweet side. He also has the most kissable lips I've ever seen." I threw that last bit in just to shock her. It did the trick. Karen's face was priceless.

"You kissed him?"

"No. But I'm thinking about it." Again, a little bravado on my part, but she was no longer thinking about Ryan.

A maroon Buick slowed and turned into Kitty's drive. "There she is." I started the Honda and slowly crept past the house. Our field of vision was narrow because of the tall hedges that enclosed the yard. Kitty pulled into the attached garage and the door descended before we could see what she was wearing. We still didn't know if she was the woman in black.

"Now what?" I asked as I drove on around the block.

"Candy bars, potato chips and pop to soothe our disappointment," Karen said.

I kept turning left and when we came to Kitty's street again I had a new

idea. I rounded the corner and turned into her drive. Karen tensed up.
"She's going to see us."

"Watch that front window," I said. I revved the engine twice.

"What are you doing?" Karen asked in horror.

I pointed toward the large front picture window. "There she is."

Kitty, searching to see what was going on in her drive, came to the window. She'd removed the sun glasses but she was still wearing that ridiculous hat. Karen and I looked away, as if we hadn't even noticed her. I put the Honda in reverse. I was just someone using the drive to turn around.

I cruised town while we talked.

"Cindy would have been one pissed widow if she'd realized her husband's mistress was at the funeral," Karen said. "I can understand why Kitty decided to hide herself in that god awful outfit."

Part of me still hoped Grant had had a legitimate reason to be in contact with Kitty, yet the affair scenario helped give Kitty motive for murder. It would cast doubt on any case Ryan could make against Cindy. "Just because we think it's a possibility Kitty and Grant were having an affair doesn't make it so," I said. "Kitty being at the funeral supports the theory, but doesn't prove it. We need more evidence, something that makes Kitty a more viable suspect."

Karen sat back in the passenger seat, her face thoughtful. "If we prove the affair, it'll break Cindy's heart," she said.

"I know. It bothers me too, but broken hearts heal in time. A murder sentence is forever."

"Yeah," Karen said. "If they *were* having an affair, and Grant went to Kitty's to break it off after Cindy confronted him, Kitty might have snapped."

I went with it. "Maybe they were in the kitchen when Grant told her, and Kitty went crazy and stabbed him in the neck with the knife."

"Then how did Grant get to the side yard?" Karen asked.

That was a problem. I thought about it for a few seconds and mused, "Maybe he didn't die right away."

"I get it," Karen said. "He staggers out of the house looking for help and dies in the side yard."

That made sense. "Then Kitty cleans up the kitchen and goes to her mom's in Marshalltown."

"Right," Karen said, "and the only people who can substantiate her alibi are her family."

"It'd be the second time Grant had strung her along and then broke it off. Both times for Cindy."

"That could push a girl over the edge," Karen said. "And all this talk about stabbing people makes me anxious, and being anxious makes me hungry."

She was exasperating. "I've asked you to stop with the food."

"I wasn't finished. I know how to take care of the food fetish."

"Good. What's the magic cure?"

"Shopping. Let's go to the mall."

"I can't. I'm worried about Ruby. I should get home and look for her." I pointed the Honda toward home. "How's Hazel? Have you heard anything from the lab?"

"Hazel's better. I think we scared Albert when he found us going through the refrigerator. I haven't heard from the lab yet. The testing's really expensive and it costs more for each poison you want them to test for. I went to the library to check on poison symptoms, and diarrhea, weakness, and vomiting were all listed as symptoms of arsenic, so that's what I'm having them look for."

"This is crazy," I said. "How can we have two killers running amuck in Alta Grove?"

Karen put the funeral handout in her purse and gathered her belongings. "For sure we have one," she said. "Someone killed Grant Waveland. As for Albert, he's just plain nuts. I wouldn't put anything past him. The minute Jean Ann told me he had a plan to get them out of debt, I got seriously worried for Hazel. How else is he going to get the money?"

"Maybe he's found a job?"

Karen smirked. "Albert's not going to get a job. He was thrilled when he

turned sixty-two and could apply for
Social Security. Besides, it would cut
in on his gambling time."

#

Karen took off as soon as we got to
my place. I hoped she wasn't making a
run to Quick Trip for candy bars. I
walked around the outside of the house,
calling for Ruby. I'd gone full circle
when John came out of his house with my
cat in his arms.

"John. I'm so sorry. Was Ruby in
your flower bed again?"

"No, I found her in my house. I
don't know how she got in."

"She's pretty sneaky," I said.
"She must have slipped inside when you
went out for something. She misses
Michelle and Ron."

"The couple I rent the house from?"

I relieved him of Ruby, and happy
to see she was safe, cuddled her in my
arms. "Yes," I said, "They used to take
care of Ruby any time I left town.
She's used to running back and forth
between the houses."

John sneezed. "I don't mean to be
a crank about your cat." He took a
hanky from his back pocket, sneezed into
it twice more, and held it to his nose
until he thought the fit was over.
"Look," he said, "It's not that I don't
like the cat." He sneezed again.

My last reservations about John
fell away. I smiled. "You're allergic
to cats, aren't you?"

"Yes. They give me itchy eyes and

a terrible headache that hangs on for hours."

"I'm so sorry. I promise to be more diligent about keeping Ruby in. I have a spray allergen reducer. I'll go get it for you. If you spray every place Ruby's been it'll help your allergies."

He sneezed once more.

"I'll be right back," I said.

I dumped Ruby in the house, grabbed the allergen reducer and went back out to John. "I'd be glad to spray your house for you," I offered.

John's eyes were rimmed in red but he managed a smile. "Great. I'm not sure I'd know how to use it." He started to rub his eyes.

"Don't touch your face. You'll make it worse."

John opened the door for me. I stepped into the heavenly scent of fresh bread. John had been baking again.

"Wash your hands," I said. "Was Ruby in the house for long?"

"I have no idea. I found her in the living room. She was making herself at home on the sofa."

While John washed up I sprayed everything in the living room. When he returned I was spraying the dining room carpet. He leaned against the arch between the two rooms, watching me. His jeans were snug, clearly defining his muscular legs and flat stomach. His shirt was tucked neatly into the waistband.

For a brief Harlequin moment I envisioned myself slowly pulling John's shirt free. I tried to hold back a silly grin, but lost control. To hide my expression, I bent over a dining room chair to rub the spray into the fabric. "That should do it." I stood and turned to John. He was smiling. I thought about myself bent over the chair with my rear end hanging in the air, and flushed. I wasn't the only one having a Harlequin moment.

He pulled his body from his stance against the wall with easy grace. "Thanks," he said. "Have you had lunch?"

"No. I spent the morning at a funeral and just got home."

"Come on. I need to get out of the house while that allergen reducer does its job. I'll take you to Wellsburg for a tenderloin sandwich."

#

My sister's divorced. She thinks the reason her husband left her is because she got fat. In the first place, our whole family is fat. If her husband had had a brain in his head he would've realized Beth was going to get fat. I don't think that's the reason he left. I think he left because my sister's a bitch.

I was no Skinny Minnie when Harry and I met. He knew what he was getting. Some women think they don't have dates because they're fat. That's not it. It's how you feel about yourself.

Sure, there are men who'll never be attracted to a plus-size woman. I don't hold it against them. After all, I could never sleep with a noodle-back. I might like and admire a noodle-back, love talking with him, love his humor, but when it comes to sex with a skinny man, no way.

But there are plenty of women who love men built like string beans and, lucky for me, there are men who like the sensual softness of a big woman. I was beginning to think John was one of those men.

He took me to the Town House for their famous tenderloin sandwich. The tenderloin is a Midwest masterpiece, a slice of pork loin with breading and spices pounded into the meat, and then deep fat fried. It's served on a hamburger bun, but the meat hangs out at least an inch all around.

It was heaven.

I was eating one of the world's best sandwiches in the company of an exceptionally good-looking man. I ate slowly, savoring the food and the company.

John took a bite of his sandwich, "Nothing like this in San Francisco," he said appreciatively. "Mom used to try making tenderloins but they didn't taste half as good."

"Do you miss your family in San Francisco?" I asked.

"I'm from a small family. My dad died of lung cancer just after my sister was born. I was ten. Mom died about six months ago. She was my last tie to San Francisco. That's why I felt free to start over here in Iowa."

"I'm terribly sorry, John. My Harry died last year. It's not easy, but time does help. Were you and your mother close?"

"Yes. She was living with me when she died."

"What happened? Was she ill?"

"Our family suffered too many tragedies. My mother was diminished with each blow." He swiveled a French fry in a pool of ketchup on his plate as he thought about the question. "I don't think she had the will to live any longer."

"How terrible for her, and for you too."

He brushed my comment aside. "Let's talk about something happier. Tell me about the funeral," he said with a grin.

I'm not usually so loose-lipped, but I wanted to entertain John, take him away from sad thoughts. "Actually," I said, "there was a funny happening at the funeral." I told him about Kitty's appearance in her weird outfit.

"I'm fascinated," he said. "Didn't you find Waveland's body in her yard?"

"Yep, that's the one."

"Do you know this Kitty well?"

"Not really. She works in the office at the high school and I'm a retired school librarian. You may not know this, but schools are a hotbed of gossip and political intrigue." I set my sandwich on the plate, trying to slow down my eating and give John a chance to catch up. Eating too fast is a hard habit to break. "Kitty's a little short in the morals department," I continued. "She gave us plenty to talk about. She even had a fling with the dearly departed, Grant Waveland."

"That's why she was at the funeral?"

"Maybe, but I wonder if they'd recently started seeing one another again."

John was taken with the gossip. "Really?" he said with a smile. "I'm beginning to understand why gossip is a favorite pastime in Alta Grove. Scandal's a lot more interesting when you know the people involved."

#

It was after two in the afternoon when John and I got home from Wellsburg. My stomach was full and I was tired. I got a pillow and Harry's favorite blanket, a lightweight fleece with cowboy print, and curled up on the Davenport. It wasn't long before Ruby joined me.

My intention was to nap, but my thoughts jumped from Hazel and Albert to Kitty and Cindy and ended up with Ryan and John. I couldn't decide what was going on with John. Was he interested in me? He was certainly attractive, and at times I was drawn to him.

Then there was Ryan. Since Karen had noticed too, maybe I'd been right about his flirting with me. I snickered. "That's just silly," I said aloud. The very idea of two good looking guys being interested in me was just plain ridiculous, wishful thinking on my part, because my body was coming to life after a year of grieving for Harry.

I'd forgotten how fascinating life could be. For months my senses had been deadened by depression. I'd probably been coming back to myself so slowly I hadn't noticed, but the night we donned the black outfits and spied on Albert I'd really felt the change. I was myself again.

As for finding Grant's body, I should have been scared silly. I should have been horrified. Instead, it made me glad to be alive, even if Harry wasn't.

#

Eventually I dozed off, and it was after three in the afternoon when I stirred. Ruby woke too. She arched her back and yawned so big I could see all her needle-sharp teeth. I rubbed her cheeks. "If you were a dog I'd take you for a walk," I told her. I'd actually tried to train Ruby to the leash with minor success, but she had never learned to enjoy it. I'd take the walk on my own.

The afternoon sun and good old Iowa humidity was beastly. People get tired of hearing, *It's not the heat, it's the humidity*, but once you've experienced an Iowa summer you understand why it's such an oft repeated phrase.

After a half mile of walking my hair was damp with sweat. I kept wiping my forehead with my shirt tail to keep the salty drips out of my eyes. The only sane decision was to forget the exercise and get back home to the air conditioning before I melted.

A green pickup drove toward me. Albert Minnert did a double-take as he passed, whipped the truck into a nearby drive, and parked.

I was startled. I glanced back when the truck door slammed. Albert was bearing down on me, fast.

"What are you doing here?" he asked. His gold-flecked brown eyes were narrow, lips drawn thin.

"Taking a walk. What does it look like?"

"Sure you are. You're just out for a stroll past my house, in this heat. I know what you're up to. You're spying on me again."

"I'm not spying on anyone." I said this with an innocent face, like I'd never dream of spying on anyone. "I didn't even realize I was on your street until you turned in the drive."

Albert's face was red with heat and anger. I felt a cold prickle of fear run up my back. I worked at breathing evenly. "But you're right," I said. I hoped agreeing with him would defuse his anger. "This heat is terrible. That's why I'm headed home." I started to walk away.

Albert grabbed my upper arm. "You and my sneaky sister-in law are up to something and I know it. Don't think you can fool me. I'm watching both of you. Stay away from my house and stay away from my stepmother."

I twisted to pull my arm from his grasp. "Don't touch me, Albert. Karen and I were simply checking to be sure Hazel had recovered from her fall at the coffee house."

Albert took a step toward me. His face was just inches from mine. I could see the glistening spittle on his lip. "You'd better stay out of my business or someone might find *you* with a knife in your throat."

It was all I could do to keep my voice steady. "Are you saying you killed Grant Waveland?"

Albert snorted. "I'm saying that two-bit lawyer got what he deserved. He won't be interfering with anyone else's marriage, will he?"

Albert's huge hand reached out and grabbed my chin. He held my face in a viselike grip, his fingers sinking into the flesh of my cheek on one side, his thumb on the other. He squeezed. "Bad things happen to people who don't mind their own business."

I held his eyes with mine and brought my knee up to his crotch. Hard. Albert's hand fell away from my face and went to cradle his family jewels as he faded to his knees in pain. I'd never before had to physically defend myself. The fact that I'd put Albert on the ground stunned me.

He looked up with hate in his eyes and pain in his voice. "Bitch," he croaked. "This isn't the end of it."

CHAPTER NINE

By the time I got home I'd quit shaking and anger had taken the place of fear. Who did that jerk think he was? Hannibal Lector? Albert had counted on my being so scared I'd keep my mouth shut, and heaven knows I was scared, but after I'd kneed him he wouldn't be so sure I'd be cowed to silence.

Next time I ran up against Albert, he'd be ready. I wouldn't get the chance to strike back. I wasn't going to wait around for him to make another move.

I called Sara and told her I was picking Karen up and we'd be at her place in twenty minutes. I told Karen all about my confrontation with Albert during the drive to Sara's place, and by the time we got there, Karen was as steamed as I was.

Poor Sara got an ear full. We sat in the kitchen, at the round oak table that had been Bruce's grandmothers, with tall glasses of iced tea with fresh lemon wedges stuck on the edge of the glass.

"I still can't believe you kneed Albert's crotch," Sara said. "I'd be hysterical if he'd grabbed me."

"Me too, if I'd thought about it. It was more like a knee jerk reaction," I said with a smile. Sara gave me a blank stare and Karen just shook her head, but I saw the corner of her mouth twitch.

I removed my lemon slice from the glass rim and squeezed its juice into my tea. "I think I should go to Ryan with this. If I don't report him, Albert's going to think he can assault me anytime he wants, and get away with it."

Sara twisted her mouth to one side before she spoke. "You're right, especially if he murdered Grant."

"He didn't actually say that. He said Grant got what he deserved and he won't be interfering with anyone else's marriage."

Karen sat her tea down and stared at me. "He said that?"

"Yes. I guess you were in the bathroom when I got to that part."

"Remember when I told you Albert cheated on Jean Ann?" she asked.

Sara and I said we remembered.

"I've kept quiet because Jean Ann asked me to, but Kitty was the woman Albert was seeing. Jean Ann forgave him, but before she did, she talked to

Grant about a divorce. Grant told her
she'd get an excellent settlement
because a friend of Jean Ann's had seen
Albert and Kitty holding hands and
kissing at a restaurant in Waterloo."

"Oh for heaven's sake," Sara said.
"Why did Jean Ann go back to him?"

Karen shook her head. "Don't ask
me. I'm no therapist."

Sara topped off our tea. "Margaret
has to talk to Ryan, but what if he
wants to know why the two on you were
visiting Hazel, and what if he finds out
we were window peeking?"

"Forget that," I said. "We don't
have to mention anything about spying
that night. Albert can't prove we're
the peepers. All we have to do is play
dumb with Ryan."

Sara rolled her eyes. "I just know
we're going to be found out."

"Will you get off that," I said.
"As for visiting Hazel, I took her to
the hospital when she fell at the coffee
shop. It's only natural that I'd check
in to see how she's doing."

Karen agreed. "And I happened to be
with Margaret when she decided to stop.
Hazel is my sister's mother-in-law so
why wouldn't I be interested in her
health?"

Sara was feeling better. "You're
right. That does sound like a good
reason to be there; and after all it's
the truth. We are concerned with
Hazel's health."

"You have nothing to worry about,"

Karen said. "Your name won't even come
up. Albert doesn't even know you were
there."

"Okay, we're agreed," I said.
"I'll go see Ryan and tell him what
happened this afternoon."

"Do you want me to come with you?"
Karen asked.

"No. I'm the one Albert
threatened. I don't want you involved.
If I go alone, Jean Ann can't blame
you."

"We should have the lab results on
Hazel's food any day now. If they find
arsenic, Jean Ann's going to have to
know what I've been up to."

"We'll cross that bridge when we
get to it," I said.

Sara leaned closer and looked at my
face. "Oh heavens! Karen, look at
Margaret's cheeks. That monster left
finger shaped bruises on her face."

Ryan wasn't in his office. I could
have talked to one of the deputies but I
didn't have the energy. I'd been wound
tight since my encounter with Albert and
now I was zapped. I left a message for
Ryan to contact me and drove home.

Ruby met me at the door and rolled
onto her back, mewing for attention. I
picked her up for a cuddle and a kiss.
What would I do without her?

Harry had been an affectionate man.
He never passed my chair without
touching my shoulder, and he liked to
hold hands when we sat on the sofa to

watch TV in the evening.

I never said it, but I thought he was a little silly about that stuff. But now that he's gone I find myself doting over Ruby, craving her affection and the feel of her rough tongue on my cheek or hand. The sting of tears tightened my face like I'd sucked on a lemon. I paced the room with Ruby in my arms, rocking her like a child. *Where's all this coming from?* I wondered. Ruby was probably asking herself the same thing. She struggled and I set her free.

When Harry was alive we'd argue about his recliner. I thought it was too big for the room and he thought it was just right for comfort. Now I was the one who found comfort in the big old chair.

What a day. Catching Kitty in that hokey Hollywood incognito getup; the run in with Albert seemed nightmarish. Lunch with John was the only sane thing I'd done in the last ten hours.

I picked up the television remote control and clicked the 'on' button. Marie was chastising Robert while Raymond smirked. Ruby jumped into my lap, looked the situation over, then curled into a ball for a nap.

I watched a second comedy rerun before I was driven to the kitchen for food. I felt empty. Empty is different than hungry. For me, feeling empty emotionally foreshadows binge eating, and right then I wanted salt and sugar and plenty of it.

I took stock of the cupboards. Tuna, green beans, old fashion oatmeal, organic peanut butter, I could feel myself panic like a smoker discovering he's out of cigarettes. I needed cupcakes with plenty of trans-fats and high fructose corn syrup, Diet Pepsi with aspartame, potato chips.

Where is my purse? There it was on the kitchen table. I slipped on my shoes and, car keys in hand, started for the door with every intention of filling a basket at the grocery store with anything that had red dye and a massive dosage of preservatives.

One tiny sliver of reason yelled in my brain. *Stop the insanity!* I pictured Susan Powter, mom's old diet guru, in her platinum blonde crew-cut, shaking her finger at me. "Put the keys down," she said in my head.

I shook off the image, but took Susan's advice. If I still wanted junk food in ten minutes I'd go to the store. *It's like giving up cigarettes,* I told myself. *If you wait out the initial flood of desire you'll be okay.*

I went to the bathroom and got the Sudoku puzzle book I keep near the toilet, sat at the kitchen table and concentrated on filling in the grid of numbers. When I looked up again, twenty minutes had passed and so had the overwhelming urge to binge.

Bacon, eggs and toast sounded reasonable. It'd also be fast. I was pulling everything from the refrigerator

THE FAT WOMAN MYSTERY

when the doorbell rang.

Ryan was standing on the porch, staring off toward the hummingbird feeder. When I opened the door he turned to me with that unforgettable smile: white even teeth, crinkles at the corner of his deep blue eyes, and the hint of a dimple on his right cheek. He brushed the hair off his forehead with his right hand. I loved that combination of dark brown hair and blue eyes.

"The deputy said you wanted to talk to me," he said.

"Yes." I opened the door wider so he could step in. "Do you mind coming to the kitchen? I'm cooking. Have you eaten?"

"Not since noon."

"It's just bacon and eggs. I wish I had—"

"Potato chips?" he asked with another of those electric smiles.

I laughed. "Guess some things never change. That's exactly what I wanted. Then I'd fix BLT's. A few cupcakes wouldn't hurt either. Like maybe six."

"Rough day?" Ryan asked.

"That's what I want to talk to you about." I put the bacon on the plastic microwave rack and turned a burner on under my iron skillet. "Scrambled all right?" I asked.

"Great. I'll make the toast."

I got the butter and bread from the

cupboard and set them next to the
toaster. The shared intimacy of
preparing a meal ignited a little spark
that sizzled through my belly. *What's
with me and men lately?* I wondered.
Was I going to be one of those *hot to
trot* widows?

The bacon was cooking in the
microwave. I added a bit of milk to the
eggs and whipped them up while the
skillet hissed and threw off fumes of
hot oil. Ryan found the plates and
silverware and set the table.

I turned around to face him. "The
napkins are in the drawer under the
silverware," I said.

His eyes studied my face and I
self-consciously turned to the stove and
poured the eggs in the skillet.

Ryan came near. "What's on your
cheek?"

"That's … part of what I want to
talk to you about."

"Are those bruises?"

"Yes, I'm bruised."

The toast popped up and the
microwave dinged. "Take care of the
toast. I'll get the bacon"

"I'd forgotten how bossy you are.
Let me see your face."

I looked up. He took my chin in
his hand and gently turned my face from
side to side. "Who?" he asked.

"Albert Minnert."

"I'll kill the creep."

"I think killing him is a little
over the top for a couple bruises.

Besides, I've already punished Albert. I kneed him." Ryan grinned and I turned to stir the eggs and to hide how much I relished his approval. "Get the toast," I said. "Let's eat."

Bacon and eggs never tasted so good. It was strange to have Ryan with me. Old feelings sputtered like a fire that had never completely died, and each time I saw him the embers were fanned and grew hotter.

Ryan stared at my face while he chewed on the toast. "Are you ready to tell me what's going on with Albert?" he asked.

"Albert's mad at me because he found me visiting at his stepmother's."

"Why would that upset him?"

"Hazel collapsed in the coffee shop and I took her to the doctor. When I stopped to see how she was doing, Albert thought I had ulterior motives."

"Did you?"

I scooped up a forkful of eggs and filled my mouth as a delaying tactic.

"Does this have anything to do with the window peeking episode?" Ryan asked.

I munched on toast, considering before I answered. "Did Albert say I was window peeping?"

"No, but we both know you were at Hazel's that night."

"Are you going to help me or not?"

"Go on with your story."

Ryan listened with narrowed eyes while I told him about Albert squeezing my face.

"You don't have to be scared," he
said. "He won't touch you again."

There was too much intensity in
Ryan's voice. I set my fork down and
looked at him. "You wouldn't do
anything stupid, would you?"

Ryan's blue eyes were cold. He
tore off a piece of toast. "That's up
to Albert."

I'd forgotten this side of Ryan's
personality. He had a dangerous quality
that could put you on edge. "I don't
think Albert's right in the head," I
said. "He's full of anger. Please
watch yourself around him."

Ryan wiped his mouth with the
napkin. "Anything else I should know?"

"Yes. I don't want to press
charges. Karen and Jean Ann are close.
If I hurt Jean Ann, I hurt Karen too.
Can you take care of this without
charging him?"

Ryan tossed the napkin on his plate
and pushed it aside. His forehead
creased in thought. Finally he said,
"I'll pay an unofficial call on Albert."

"Thanks. Listen, I have something
else to tell you about Albert." I told
him about Kitty and Albert's affair, and
how Albert hated Grant because Jean Ann
had gone to him about a divorce. "Karen
says Albert was furious with Grant. I
know it's a wild idea, but do you think
he could have killed Grant?"

"I don't know but I'm sure going to
look into it." He stood. "I want you

to stay away from Albert. Let me handle him. Stay away from Hazel's too. I don't know what kind of cloak and dagger stuff you girls have going, but I want you to end it."

I sucked in my lower lip so he wouldn't see the smile. I felt safer knowing Ryan would look after me. On the other hand, he wasn't going to order me around. Not even Harry had ever been able to tell me what to do. I had a mind of my own and I intended to use it.

At the door, Ryan turned. "Dinner was good. It reminded me of when we were kids and you'd fix us bacon and eggs after we got home from the movies."

Another gust of oxygen stirred the fire. The sweet memory of the two of us at sixteen, cooking in mom's kitchen, overflowed in my heart. How sad to know I was too experienced at life to ever again give love so completely. "Yes," I said softly, "those were innocent years."

Ryan's voice was quiet too. "I often think about the way we were together Maggie."

He stepped into the dusky evening, and I stood watching until his car was out of sight.

CHAPTER TEN

Two Hundred and five pounds.

I hadn't lost a single ounce. I'd
hoped for more, but then I always hope
for more. I was down two pounds for the
week with one day to go before the
meeting. I decided to be happy with
that. I stepped off the scales and
brushed my teeth.

What I wanted was a miracle, a
genie in my toothpaste to pop out of the
tube when I squeezed. He'd look like a
bald Hagrid, wearing a tiny vest on his
big body, and voluminous pants. There'd
be a squiggle of toothpaste on his head,
like the curlicue on top of a Dairy
Queen cone. Arms folded across his
chest, he'd bow, thank me for releasing
him from his toothpaste tube prison, and
reward me with three wishes.

I'd wish first for a lovely, slim
body; second, for the beginnings of the
wattle under my chin to be gone; and
third . . . maybe I'd think about that
one for a while. I didn't want to be
careless with the last wish.

Even without three wishes, this was

a brand new day. I could let it unfold naturally or set goals and take care of something on my 'to do' list.

After my shower I put on fresh pajamas, the pair with Disney princesses in ball gowns. It was going to be hot. The weatherman said the temperature in Alta Grove would reach the mid-nineties, a good day to stay inside with the air on.

I browsed through the bookshelf. A mystery sounded good. I'd start reading after breakfast, and maybe later I'd buy one of those 'On Demand' movies on TV.

I decided on oatmeal. I'd have some orange juice and toast too. The decision to excuse myself from all chores made me feel lighter. Maybe if I let the place go to wrack and ruin I'd never have to diet again. I could let the garbage build up like Sarah Cynthia Sylvia Stout.

I was considering my favorite line in the Silverstein poem about Sara Stout: *Cellophane from green baloney, rubbery blubbery macaroni*, when the phone rang.

Another ring.

Whoever it is, I won't answer, I told myself, . . . *three ring-a-dingees*. Mom always said I was born curious. I checked caller ID. *Four ring-a-dingees*. It was Karen. She might have the report on Hazel's food.

I poked the answer button. "Hello. Did you hear from the lab?"

"No." Karen was impatient. "For

SANDRA NOBLE

heaven's sake, Margaret, we got the
samples from Hazel on Sunday, I took it
in on Monday, and this is just Tuesday
morning. It's not like I'm a crime
scene investigator. I can't put a rush
on it."

"You're right. I'm just anxious
about Hazel."

Karen rushed on, "I don't think we
have to worry about that right now. I
called to tell you about Jean Ann's call
last night. I don't know what you said
to Ryan but it worked. Jean Ann said
Ryan came to the door and asked Albert
to step outside. Albert was gone for
about five minutes, and when he came
back, Jean Ann said he tried to act all
cocky, like there was nothing wrong, but
she knew he was scared."

"Ryan's been issuing warnings here
too," I said. "We've been ordered to
stay away from Albert, and from Hazel's
place too."

"Did he say anything about Kitty
Samuels being at the funeral?"

"He doesn't know about that little
escapade, and I don't plan on telling
him. He'd just be angry with me for
poking around in his investigation."

"I've been thinking about Kitty.
Why do you suppose she went to such
lengths to go to Grant's funeral?"

"You know what they say. 'Love is
lovelier the second time around. If
they got back together after nearly four
years apart, maybe she really did love
him."

124

"Hard to believe Kitty's capable of
such deep and abiding feelings."
Karen's voice fell to a whisper. "Gotta
go," she said. "I'm at the office and
the Buchwald's just walked in. They've
been calling about the Ames house."

I curled up in Harry's chair and
opened the mystery novel, but my mind
kept returning to Karen's call. Where
did Kitty fit into Grant's murder? She
had to have something to do with it. It
was just too much of a coincidence for
his body to end up in her yard."

I couldn't remember the last time
I'd talked to her. It was probably the
spring, when I'd gone through my
weightlifting phase. The school opens
their fitness room to the public early
in the morning and after four o' clock
in the afternoon.

I went several times a week until
my kids came home for Easter. Since
then I've had a million excuses, but the
bottom line is, I never went back.
Kitty's probably getting close to forty
and she has a nice body. At her age a
pretty body doesn't come without paying
a big price in the gym.

School would start in a few weeks.
That meant the office people were
already back to work. Maybe I *would* set
a goal for today. I'd been thinking
about getting back to weight training.
No time like the present.

#

At three-thirty I went upstairs to
find my workout clothes. A pair of red

cut-off sweats and a black tee-shirt
with a YMCA logo. After I dressed I
dabbed a bit of make-up on my cheeks to
hide the bruises.

The school fitness room regulars
were a mixture of high school athletes,
senior citizens that used the gym as a
social center, and a sprinkling of
thirty to fifty year olds working
seriously to hold back time.

Kitty was on a treadmill, walking
with the machine set on a steep incline,
and pumping her arms. She was the only
person in the room with authentic
workout clothing: tight spandex black
pants to the knee, a body-hugging pink
shirt that embraced her generous bust,
and a pink and white sweatband to hold
her impossibly red hair away from her
face.

I stepped on the treadmill next to
hers. Kitty wasn't especially glad to
see me. She gave me a cool glance, and
without missing a step said, "Looks like
you could use a workout, Margaret."

That woman was in shape. If I were
walking that fast I wouldn't be able to
breathe, let alone talk. I gritted my
teeth, ignored the put down, and tried
for a friendly tone. "You, on the other
hand, look great, Kitty. It's obvious
you're in top condition."

That earned me a brief smile.
"Thanks," she said. "It's getting
harder every year." She lowered the
incline level to start the cool-down
stage of her cardio workout. "Have you

been enjoying your five minutes of fame, Margaret?"

Guess it would take more than compliments to make Kitty believe I gave a damn about her workout secrets. "You mean because I found Grant's body?" I asked innocently.

She looked at me with narrowed eyes, "Yes, but what I'd really like to know is, what the hell were you doing in my yard?"

You know, that woman was actually intimidating. My instinct was to step back from her glare, but I forced myself to show only calm assurance, on the surface anyway. I stood my ground and answered. "It was just a fluke. I'd gone for a walk and got tired so I cut through your yard to get home faster." Now I tried for a friendlier footing, sort of a 'good cop' approach. "Finding the body was certainly a shock. I'm sure it was for you too. I mean, there was a time you and Grant were close. It must have been awful, having his body dumped on your property and all."

Kitty slowed her machine again. I could feel the chill in the air.

"It's been years since Grant and I were an item."

I know the old saying about honey and vinegar, but there was no way Kitty and I would ever be friends and we both knew it, so I dropped all pretenses and went for the throat. "Some people say your husband left you because of that relationship. Bet you were mad as hell when Grant dropped you for Cindy."

She got off the treadmill and wiped her face with the towel that hung around her neck. "That is old news. No one cares about that after all these years."

"So you and Grant were on good terms?"

Kitty placed her hands, rolled into fist, at each side of her tiny waist, and spoke in clipped tones. "We weren't on any terms at all. He got married and that was that."

"Really? Then why, after all this time, did you go to his funeral?"

She sputtered. "I didn't."

"I saw you there in that silly costume."

"I don't know what you're talking about," Kitty hissed.

She walked away. I shut my machine down and followed. "It's nothing to me if you went to the funeral," I said. "Finding the body has just made me more curious than usual."

Kitty's voice went shrill. "More curious than usual? That's impossible, Margaret. You've always been like a dog with a bone."

"I'm also curious as to why you were driving by Grant and Cindy's house so often. Were you stalking Grant?"

Kitty glared at me, trying to look tough, but her eyes told a different story. They darted about, showing her nerves.

"Just remember, Margaret, curiosity *killed* the cat."

She swished off to the locker room. I'd definitely upset her, but I couldn't figure it out. Was it because she was the killer, or was she afraid of something?

#

John Gildenbond called to me as I opened my back door. "Margaret, wait up. I've been trying to get a hold of you."

Why did he always catch me looking like something the cat dragged in? I felt ridiculous in my chopped-off sweats and tee-shirt, but I turned and gave him my best smile. "I've been working out," I said, by way of apology. "Do you want to come in?"

"No, I just wanted to invite you for dinner. I'm planning salmon with cucumber sauce, twice baked potatoes, and green beans. I bought the beans fresh at the farmers' market. It's going to be too good to eat without an appreciative guest."

"John, I'm impressed: scones, BLT's, and now an amazing salmon dinner. Yes, I'd love to come."

"Great, see you at six?"

#

There were four bags of tomatoes on the kitchen cupboard. Sara must have dropped them off. I hadn't planned on preserving any food this season, but I'd have to deal with this unexpected bounty.

For several years before Harry died I'd been on a health food kick. I mean

health food. I canned and froze veggies
from Sara's organic garden, made my own
apple sauce and baked with sugarless
recipes.

I'd go to the Plunket farm, where
chickens run around crapping all over
the yard, to buy eggs, chicken, and pork
because they'd been raised without
hormone or antibiotic injections.

High fructose corn syrup and trans-
fats were banned from the house, and I
cooked every meal from scratch. My body
was my temple and, like it or not, Harry
had to eat the temple food too.

He went along with my zealous
guardianship of our physical wellbeing
because things like homemade noodles,
even if they were made with whole wheat
flour, made up for the pain of Ding Dong
withdrawal.

When Harry died I started eating.
I ate my way through the funeral
arrangements, the consoling calls, and
the little family dramas that occurred
as a consequence. I ate until I grew
out of my clothing.

I fell into the trap of believing I
should be punished for gaining weight,
and shopped at discount stores, and even
the dollar stores, for inexpensive
summer clothing in my new larger size.
I didn't feel worthy of anything nicer.
Besides, being this fat was to be a very
temporary condition.

Calling a halt to the binges wasn't
that easy. More and more junk food
found its way into my kitchen. I even

stopped for fast food several times. Finally, a couple of weeks ago, I reached rock bottom of my fall from organic grace.

I'd made a grocery list; not a single healthy item made the top ten. I wanted potato chips, cupcakes, and Pepsi. I spent a fortune on sugar and salt. When Sara stopped by later that day she found me in a morose state of mind, eating from the bag of potato chips in my lap.

She didn't scold. Instead she sat next to me on the davenport, talked of the PTA fundraiser, and told me all about a funny little squabble she was having with Bruce. She showed up again the next day, then the next. I knew she was very concerned for me, and I didn't want her to be worried.

The next day I went through my stash of food and threw out everything that wasn't good for me. Actually, there wasn't a whole lot to toss after the monumental binge.

I hadn't been able to wear anything but my discount store clothing in months, but I wanted to dress for dinner with John. Not heels and nylons. I didn't want to go that far. But I wanted to look good and it was time to retouch the makeup to hide the faint bruise on my cheek.

I went upstairs and stood in front of the closet. Ruby followed me and sat on her haunches staring at the clothes alongside me. I flipped through the

hangers. No, too small. No, too long.
No, too bright. No . . . well, maybe.
I pulled out a blue print skirt with an
elastic waist and a flounce at the
bottom. "What do you think, Ruby?"

Ruby answered with a mew and I took
it as a *yes*.

Clinton and Stacy say you can
balance a smaller bottom half with a
larger top half by wearing a skirt that
flares. They also hate elastic waist
bands, but what do they know about
having a waist as large as your hips?
This skirt could work. I found a navy
blue camisole and a white blouse to wear
over it.

I checked the clock. I had an
hour. Why does it take so much time to
be beautiful and so little to be ugly to
the bone?

CHAPTER ELEVEN

John stared for an extra beat when he opened his door. Those sensuous full lips curved in a slow show of appreciation. "You look lovely, Margaret."

He stepped slightly aside to let me in but my body had to brush against his to pass. A tingle of womanly awareness warmed my belly.

The dining room table was covered with a pink and aqua plaid tablecloth with matching napkins. The plates were white bone china with a gold rim, and two crystal candle holders held white tapers.

John lit the candles and I melted right alongside them when he pulled my chair out to seat me. "This is elegant," I said.

He bent and kissed my head. "So are you."

"I don't think I ever met a man who appreciated crystal and china."

John's eyes danced with mirth.

"You still haven't. All these things were Mother's. I dug them out of one of the storage boxes I've been trying to sort through. What a job. It seems wrong to get rid of the things she loved, but if I don't, all that stuff's just going to gather dust in the garage and basement."

"My kids are going to have the same problem. I plan to die in my big old house and leave the mess to them. They'll just have to bring in a giant-sized dumpster when I'm gone."

John placed the food on the table. The pink salmon on the white plate with the pink and aqua plaid tablecloth was beautiful. I wondered if he had planned it that way or if it was fortuitous. He was certainly a complicated man, stern, yet tender when he talked about his mother; masculine, yet a marvel in the kitchen.

"I noticed the sheriff at your house yesterday evening. Any problem?" John asked, when he'd seated himself across from me.

I served myself a portion of salmon and handed him the platter. "Not really," I said. "I wanted to talk to him about an incident with Albert Minnert. We had a confrontation when I was out for a walk."

"I don't think I know him."

"You're bound to meet him soon. He belongs to the Senior Golf League you play in."

"Is this guy a problem for you?"

134

THE FAT WOMAN MYSTERY

I spooned green beans on my plate
and considered the question. John
sounded like another protective man. I
didn't feel like a woman in distress, so
I reassured him. "No, I just asked Ryan
to have a talk with him. It's no big
deal." I turned my attention to the
delicious food on my plate. The fish
was flakey and moist, the green beans
bright in color, seasoned with garlic
and onions, and delectable. "This is so
good, John. You're spoiling me."

"You're an appreciative guest.
It's fun to cook for you. I hate it
when a woman just plays with her food."

I laughed. "Then you've invited the
right woman to dine, and food always
taste best when someone else does the
cooking."

John used his napkin to dab at his
full, kissable lips. "I thought maybe
the sheriff was there to ask more
questions about your finding that
lawyer's body."

"No. Ryan's working hard but
doesn't seem to be getting very far.
I'm afraid Grant's wife, Cindy, is the
only real suspect right now. She's such
a sweet girl and I happen to know she
loved that jerk. No way did she kill
him. But she doesn't have an alibi."

"What about the woman who owned the
house where you found the body? There
must be some kind of rationale for the
body being in her yard."

I put my fork down, determined to
slow the pace on my eating. I didn't

want John to think I was a glutton, even if I was occasionally. "That's what I think," I said. "Especially since Cindy suspected Kitty and Grant were seeing one another again."

"Again?"

"Yes, again. Kitty and Grant had a romance years ago. At the time, school gossip was that Kitty's husband dumped her because he'd found them in bed together."

"I'm beginning to see why you suspect this woman."

"I could be wrong." I picked my fork up again and speared another morsel of salmon. I had to hand it to him; John knew his way around a stove. I savored the fish, while filling John in on another piece of Alta Grove history. "Years ago a big hunk of money was embezzled at the school. My first instinct was that Kitty was the thief, but they found evidence against another woman. She was arrested and pled guilty."

"Did you think the other woman did it?"

"Certainly not at first, but after she confessed I had to accept it. Still, Kitty is no friend of mine."

We finished the meal with easy talk about John's golf game and the new people he was meeting at the club house. I was pleased he was making a good adjustment to small town ways. He refused my offer to help clear our plates, and returned from the kitchen to set a saucer with a slim slice of cherry cheesecake in front of me.

"Oh John, that looks marvelous, but I'm trying to lose a few pounds. Would you mind if I skipped dessert?"

"Margaret, it's a very small piece, and the rest of the meal was healthy and low calorie too. Besides, I think you look perfect. Not every man's attracted to skinny women. Some of us like curves."

"That's what Harry always said."

"Harry was a man with good taste."

I'd had a couple glasses of wine with dinner so my defenses were down. I gave in and savored every bite of that cheesecake, and after, when we were cleaning the kitchen together, I said, "Next time, you can come to my place, and I'll cook. I don't have your talent in the kitchen, but I'll come up with something."

"I'd like that Margaret, but I'm afraid my cat allergy won't allow it."

I scraped my plate in the disposal side of the sink. "Have you thought about medication?"

"No. I've never had the need, but now that I have a close friend who owns a cat it's a good idea. I play golf with a Doctor Hepple. I'll call his office and make an appointment."

"Not Doctor Death."

"Who?"

"I'm talking about Doctor Hepple. I wish you'd try someone else. I don't think Hepple's all that good of a doctor."

John's eyes twinkled. "He'll do fine. I don't get very sick so I don't need a very good doctor."

"Men, you're all too macho to take care of your health." Too much anger came out with my statement.

John tilted his head and looked at me. "If it's important to you, I'll see someone else."

"I'm sorry. Who you see is none of my business. It's Harry I'm mad at. If he'd taken better care of himself he might still be with me." I hung my dishtowel on the hook to dry. "Thanks for a great evening," I said.

"You're leaving already?"

"Yes, I have tomatoes from my friend Sara's garden that need taking care of."

"Are you going to can them tonight?"

"No. I think I'll peel them and pack them in plastic bags to freeze."

"I'll walk you home."

"That's not necessary."

"I'd like to."

We walked together to my house, and when I turned to say good night, John put his hands on my waist and drew me close. His kiss was warm, his full sensual lips inviting. I kissed him back.

He grinned when he released me. "Now you know why I wanted to walk you home."

\#

I was heating water to loosen tomato skins and trying to decide how I felt about John's kiss. Was I ready for a romance? And what would happen after the romance? Could we still be good neighbors if it didn't last? When Karen called, I still hadn't made up my mind.

"I've been trying to catch you all afternoon," she said. "Where have you been?"

"At the school workout room, and then I had dinner with John Gildenbond."

"I'd better get a full report on that good-looking neighbor at Fit Girls tomorrow night."

"Really, Karen, It's nothing."

"I'll be the judge of that. The reason I called is to let you know the lab contacted me this afternoon. Thank God I didn't mention my suspicions to Jean Ann. I feel like an idiot as it is. They didn't find even a trace of arsenic in Hazel's corned beef. I don't know. Maybe Hazel did have the flu?"

"Don't feel bad, Karen. This is good news. Doctor Hepple can't be wrong every time. It must have been the flu. Did you call Sara?"

"Yeah, I got a hold of her earlier."

"Okay. I'll have to get back to freezing tomatoes. See you tomorrow evening."

#

Two hundred and four and a half pounds.

Two hundred and four and one half

pounds was my true weight. I was pleased. I'd have a two and a half pound loss to report at the meeting. I wasn't cooking. I'd spent last night and this morning dealing with tomatoes and wasn't volunteering any more time in the kitchen, but I had to go to the grocery store. The cupboards were bare. Nothing panics me like bare cupboards.

I ate breakfast and made a shopping list because two enemies of the dieter are impulse shopping and shopping hungry. When I got to the store I had just one problem, too many cups of tea with breakfast. Feeling thankful the bathroom was near the front door, I dashed in before I'd even found a good cart.

Hazel was washing her hands at the sink. I said hello and hurried into the first stall. When I finished I found Hazel still at the sink, waiting for me. She was fidgeting, moving from one foot to another. "Is there something wrong?" I asked.

"I'm so glad you're here," she said.

She was obviously upset; it took her a few seconds to speak. Finally, she announced, "I have a terrible problem and I hope you can help me."

"Of course I'll help. What is it?"

"I'm so embarrassed." Hazel started to cry. "I didn't even realize it. I was in the produce department and Sally Carson came over and whispered I had a stain on the seat of my slacks. I still didn't understand so she said she thought maybe I'd had an accident and I'd better check it out in the bathroom."

I gave Hazel a hug. We can handle this. I took off the summer sweater I always wore to the grocery store. No matter how hot it is outside, the grocery store is always freezing. I put the sweater around Hazel's butt and tied the sleeves around her waist. "This will take care of it until you get home."

"I don't know what's happening to me. I'm having so many problems with my bowels. I'm afraid to leave the house because of it, but I was out of so many things. Albert's been doing so much for me, I didn't want to ask him to handle the grocery shopping too."

"Nonsense, just give him a list. And Hazel, please make an appointment with your doctor. In the meantime you can use Depends so you don't spoil your clothes. You're going to be fine."

She gave me a quivery smile.

"I'll pick up some Depends while I'm shopping and drop them off on my way home," I said.

#

Sara and Kitty arrived for the Fit Girls meeting at the same time. We ate Subway sandwiches, took a walk, and then took our usual places in the parlor. I couldn't wait to report. Before we were even settled, I announced my weight loss.

Sara's face lit up. "That's good news," she said. "You're on your way now. Nothing will stop you now."

Karen was beaming too. "Your head's in the game, Margaret. I know you. Once you get on track you're a weight loss machine."

I proudly sucked in the praise. "I even stopped at the school's fitness room and worked out for a while."

Karen grinned. "I wonder if this new urge to get back in shape has anything to do with your handsome neighbor."

I took the question seriously. "Maybe, I do like him and his attentions certainly make life more interesting. I feel like I'm climbing out of a hole." I looked at Karen. "John is just a tiny part of it. I know you feel silly over the Albert and Hazel thing, but it was an adventure, and just what I needed to get over the hump. I really am better."

Sara agreed. "Stalking Albert was like being on a rollercoaster. Scary, but it was fun too."

"How about you, Karen?" I asked. "How was your week?"

"I'm holding tight."

Sara said, "I think you look wonderful, Karen. Most dieters regain weight, but you've held your weight loss for over two years. I don't think you'll ever get fat again."

Karen smiled, "Thanks, Sara, but I've learned where food's concerned, never say never. Right now my weight

isn't a problem. I've learned to deal
with the little frustrations without
stuffing my face and, knock on wood, I
haven't had any earth shaking events
going on in a couple years. But watch
out if something big happens, 'cause the
first thing I'll do is hit the
refrigerator."

Sara's voice was a little dejected.
"I can't even handle the small stuff.
Like today, Mom stopped by for a visit,
and after she left I ate all the snicker
doodles I'd set aside for the kids'
lunches."

I perked up. The stuff that comes
out of Sara's mom's mouth is unreal.
"What'd she say this time?"

"She asked if I'd lost weight this
week and I said I hadn't, and then she
told me if I didn't stop eating they
were going to have to bury me in a piano
box."

My chin nearly hit my chest. This
time Sara's mother had gone too far. "I
can't believe that woman. What is she
thinking?"

Sara smiled a sad smile. "She's
trying to shock me into action."

"I think you should get one of
Bruce's cattle prods and shock her,"
Karen said. "You've got to stand up for
yourself."

"She's my mother. I don't want to
be disrespectful."

Karen leaned forward and spoke
sternly, "I don't care if she's the
Queen of Sheba. You can't let her talk

to you like that."

"Maybe that should be your goal this week," I offered. "Rather than a weight loss, you can stand up to your mother."

"I don't know if I'll be able to do that."

"It's like learning to eat healthy," Karen said. "It doesn't happen overnight, but you can work toward the goal of respecting yourself."

"I promise to work at it," Sara said, trying to shift the focus to another subject. "How's Jean Ann doing on the diet pills? I'm thinking of trying them."

"She's lost a few pounds, but I'm not sure it's worth it. She says when she eats anything fatty she has to make a lot of trips to the bathroom and cross her fingers she'll make it in time."

"That doesn't sound good."

Karen rolled her eyes, "I don't think it would happen if she followed directions. The paperwork that comes with the pills says to eat low fat, but Jean Ann's eating buttered popcorn and bacon."

Sara wrinkled her nose. "Now I'm not sure. Maybe I'd better think about it for a while." She turned to me. "What's your goal for the week?"

"I'm going to lose two pounds this week and try to think of someone besides myself for a change. Cindy's in a mess and I've been holding back. I don't believe for a moment she killed Grant.

A big part of me doesn't want to get any further involved in a murder scandal, but I'm going to brave the gossip and do what my heart tells me to do."

Karen clapped her hands. "I'm with you."

"Oh my gosh," Sara gushed. "Haven't you heard? They arrested Cindy for murder this afternoon."

CHAPTER TWELVE

After a shower I put on my white PJ's with the big aqua polka-dots and climbed between the eight hundred thread count sheets I'd found on sale at Dillard's department store.

Heaven.

I closed my eyes, thinking sleep would come quickly, but thoughts of Cindy pricked at my conscience. What was she feeling tonight? I pictured her on a narrow cot, without benefit of sheets, wearing an orange jumpsuit for pajamas, covered with a rough, skinny blanket.

For the past year I'd thought of little but myself, wallowing in self-pity and donuts. As I drifted toward sleep, I comforted myself with vows to be a better friend to Cindy.

\#

I was sitting on a tree branch watching the full moon rise when it morphed and John's face floated into focus. His sensuous lips were tempting, luring me to him for a kiss. I moved in slow motion, my nightgown, (*Nightgown? Had to be a dream*) softly fluttering in the starry night.

Just as I puckered up for the kiss, John's face began to change. I drew back, watching the process. Now the moon was Harry.

Like Jack in *An American Werewolf in London*, Harry's flesh had deteriorated. I was fascinated rather than frightened. "You're not looking so good, Harry," I said.

"What can you expect after a year underground?"

"Are you here because I kissed John?"

Harry's mouth moved to answer but everything went into a slow swirl and his words were garbled. Then his face faded into the moon again and shrank into the night.

#

First thing in the morning I went to the county jail. Cindy's arrest made it even more important for me to show my support. I remembered when Alice Crowley was arrested for embezzlement. I'd felt bad for her, but like everyone else, I'd backed away after she was arrested.

Grant Waveland probably did the best he could under the circumstances, but the prosecutor's office had experts ready to testify that the unauthorized purchases made with school credit cards could be traced to Alice's computer. Her guilt was sealed when they found an

emerald ring, bought with the school's
credit card, in her jewelry box.

After the police found the ring,
Alice pled guilty. Since she'd never
even had a speeding ticket, the judge
put her on probation and ordered her to
pay restitution. Nearly seventy
thousand dollars.

I bet the embezzlement was the
first and only thing Alice had ever done
to be ashamed of. Lots of people
thought she got off easy, but I didn't
think so. The theft had cost her
everything: self-respect, her husband,
her job and her friends. I wish I'd
been brave enough to wish her well when
she left town.

Now I'm older and less concerned
with other people's opinion of me.
Life's getting shorter and I want to
feel good about myself. Cindy was my
friend and this was surely the lowest
point of her life. I wanted to stand by
her.

#

"Cindy isn't here," Ryan said. He
walked around his desk and sat. "Her
father came last night. This morning he
arranged bail."

I was furious. Just thinking about
Cindy having to spend a night in jail
made me want to slap Ryan silly. "How
could you arrest her? What evidence
could you possibly have?"

"She allowed us to search her
house."

"Of course she did," I said. "She

had nothing to hide."

"We found a blouse missing a red heart-shaped button. The buttons were identical to the one we found in Kitty's yard."

My mouth dropped. I stood soundlessly while Ryan yammered on.

"She admits she was worried Grant and Kitty were having an affair. That's motive. She has no alibi for the night Grant was killed so she had opportunity. The button proves she was in Kitty's yard, and that's enough to arrest her."

I finally found my voice. "I don't know what Cindy was doing in Kitty's yard. But she didn't kill Grant. She loved him. I was in Kitty's yard the night he was stabbed, but I sure as hell didn't do it, and neither did Cindy. You're so wrong about this."

"Cindy will have her day in court."

"Think about what you're doing, Ryan. You can't zero in on Cindy just because it's the easiest path. What about Kitty? Kitty and her husband split because she was seeing Grant, then Grant dumped her for Cindy. What woman wouldn't be furious? And then there's Albert. He hated Grant because he advised Jean Ann to divorce him."

Ryan leaned back in his chair. "I'd say Grant gave her good advice. Wouldn't you agree?"

"That has nothing to do with it. I'm saying Albert's a loose cannon and I wouldn't be a bit surprised if he got mad enough at Grant to kill him."

Ryan blew air from his lips and sat up straight in his chair. "I'm still looking at Albert and Kitty too. But the state police are involved and I had no choice but to arrest Cindy."

I turned and walked out of Ryan's office. Part of me understood his predicament, but I was too upset to be gracious.

\#

I drove straight to Cindy's.

Cindy's sister Annabelle, a paler, taller version of Cindy, let me in and invited me into the kitchen. It was a vast room with rich oak mission-style cupboards and granite countertops. Sunshine from floor to ceiling windows, on the south side of the room, set the golden tones in the cupboards aglow. Despite its size the room was warm.

"I'll leave you ladies to your visit," Annabelle said.

Cindy looked haggard. Who wouldn't after everything she'd been through lately? Not to mention a night in the county jail. The lines alongside her nose and mouth had deepened and her dark hair, thrown into a ponytail, looked like it could use a shampoo.

She gave me a hug, then poured tea into flowered mugs. "I'm so glad to see you. I was afraid everyone would believe I killed Grant after I was arrested."

"I don't believe any such thing."

"You may be the only one." There

was a catch in her voice and Cindy
turned her face away. "I'm afraid to
leave the house. I'm afraid of what
I'll see in the faces of all those
people who used to smile and greet me in
the grocery store aisles. I can almost
hear them, on their front porches, on
the phone to friends, over the fences,
talking about the news of the day. Did
you hear? Cindy Waveland was arrested
for murdering her husband."

I reached over and took her hand.
Cindy looked at me, her mouth set in a
bitter smile. "And do you know what's
funny about all this, Margaret? I
understand. I know if it were someone
other than me, I'd be talking about it
too. I'd run into Ann Jenkins at the
drug store and the two of us would get a
cup of coffee and hash over every
detail." She held fingertips to her
mouth and breathed deep to suck down her
emotions.

"If you need to cry, cry," I said.
"You don't have to be brave for me."

She sat across from me at the
table. "I don't feel brave. I'm scared
to death I'm going to spend the rest of
my life in prison, but I don't have any
tears left. I cried all night in that
jail cell. I kept thinking of Angie.
Her father's gone, and if I go to
prison, she'll grow up without either of
us."

"I know everything looks bad right
now," I said, but you're not going to
prison. Ryan will find Grant's killer,

and for now your mom's taking good care of Angie. All you have to do is take care of yourself." I said a silent prayer that all my reassurances would come true.

Cindy tried to smile. We both knew she was dangling from a slender thread. I wanted to strengthen that thread. Give Ryan and the state police someone else to consider. "What do you know about Albert Minnert?" I asked.

Cindy was surprised by the question. "Why are you asking about Albert?"

"Because he has a hot temper and Grant wasn't one of his favorite people."

"I don't know a lot about him, but you're right. He was very angry with Grant. When Albert's wife was thinking of leaving him, she went to see Grant. I only know about it because Albert called the house several times and he was angry and foulmouthed with anyone who answered the phone."

"That's Albert alright."

"Grant recorded a couple of his nasty calls, and then went to see him. He told him if he didn't quit harassing us he'd give the tapes to the police. Grant said Albert was livid, but he did quit calling."

"I wonder if he was mad enough to kill Grant."

"It's possible. The guy has a real anger management problem."

"Do you still have the tapes?" I

asked.

"I'm not sure. Do you think it's important?"

"I do. Find them and give them to your lawyer. Those tapes might convince a jury you aren't the only suspect."

I hesitated to ask the foremost question on my mind, but Cindy read my face.

"What is it?" she asked. "What are you thinking about?"

"I realize it's none of my business, but I'm wondering what you were doing in Kitty's yard."

She gave me a sheepish smile. "Remember our discussion about the Lifetime movie?"

"The one where the woman got the goods on her husband?"

"Right. The night before Grant was killed, he called to say he'd be home late. I couldn't stand it anymore. It was driving me crazy. I had to know if he was cheating. Grant's mother had Angie. I played detective and looked for his car at Kitty's."

"Me and my stupid ideas," I said. "That Lifetime movie's why I found the body. I was walking near Kitty's and had my camera, so off I went to play private eye."

Cindy pressed her fingers against her mouth like a Japanese Geisha and giggled softly. "At least you didn't run around dropping clues. I wouldn't be in this mess if I'd taken care of that button. I knew it was loose. I just hadn't gotten around to fixing it."

"Well? Did you find Grant?"

"Kitty came home but Grant never showed up. I drove past his office later and his car was in his parking slot. He was telling the truth. At least that time."

"See. It's very possible Grant and Kitty weren't having an affair."

"I'd like to believe that but I can't. His cell would ring and Grant would leave the room to take the call, or I'd walk in and he'd whisper something and hang up."

"That does sound like something was going on."

"Considering their past relationship, you can understand why I'd be suspicious. Besides, remember, I told you I'd checked his cell?"

I nodded.

"What I didn't mention was a message from Kitty that Grant hadn't gotten around to erasing."

"Did you play it?"

"All she said was, 'He called again.' I know that doesn't prove they were having an affair, but why else would he be so secretive? And why was he gone all the time?"

"I don't know. Have you considered talking to Kitty?"

"No. I'm afraid I wouldn't be able to hold myself together, and I don't want to give her the satisfaction of seeing me fall apart."

We were quiet while we each sipped

our tea.   Then Cindy set her mug down
and looked at me.   "Would you do it?   I
have to know the truth, Margaret.   Would
you talk to Kitty?"

CHAPTER THIRTEEN

I didn't promise Cindy I'd talk to Kitty. But I did say I'd consider it. She wouldn't be home from work until four o' clock. That gave me most of the day to think about it. I was a little worried about Ryan. He wasn't going to like it if I decided to see Kitty.

My stomach growled at me. Breakfast had been skimpy: peanut butter toast, a piece of sausage and a tiny glass of orange juice. It was after noon now. I opened a can of potato broccoli soup, one hundred and twenty calories per serving, and two servings per can. What a laugh. Who eats half a can of soup? Two hundred and forty calories is the true calorie count. I'd have toast and butter with it. Diet Delight whole grain bread at forty-five calories, with skinny spread butter, would make it seventy-five.

Three hundred and sixty calories. Hmmm, I could have more if I wanted. I opened the refrigerator and scanned the shelves. Nothing enticing. The cupboards didn't reveal anything interesting either so I ate the soup and toast.

The back doorbell chimed and Karen called my name. "Are you home?"

"I'm here. Come on in." Karen looked spiffy in a dressy pair of crop pants cuffed at the calf. Her white blouse looked like it had just got back from the laundry and had a light touch of starch.

"Did you have a house showing this morning?" I asked.

"Yes, but it was a waste of time. If I'm any judge, I'd say that couple's living in dreamland if they think they can qualify for a three hundred thousand dollar house." She glanced at the small kitchen table. "Maybe we should move. I hope you don't mind, but I asked Sara to meet us here."

"Of course I don't mind. What's going on?"

"Albert's what's going on."

"Yoo hoo," Sara called from the back entry. "I have gifts. I brought you each potatoes from the garden."

#

I poured everyone a cold glass of tea and we went to the parlor.

Sara sipped her tea thoughtfully, "I thought you said the food test came back negative."

"It did," Karen said, "but something's wrong." I saw Hazel at Jean Ann's before my appointment this morning. She's lost weight and she just isn't herself."

I thought Karen was right, and I told them about Hazel's problem in the grocery store. "I hope she called the doctor."

Karen nodded. "She did, and he saw her right away but didn't find anything wrong with her." "He gave her a list of high fiber foods and told her to concentrate on getting enough fiber in her diet."

"That might help," Sara said.

"Maybe," Karen said. "Hazel told me Albert comes every day to check on her. That's the part that worries me most. She's singing his praises. She said she has more money than she can spend in a lifetime, and now that she realizes what a fine man Albert's matured into she has no problem helping him and Jean Ann out."

We were all quiet for a moment while it sunk in. "So," I said. "When Albert told Jean Ann he had a plan to get cash for bills ..."

"My thoughts exactly," Karen finished.

"You've lost me," Sara said.

Karen explained. "If Albert had asked Hazel for money before she was dependent on him, she would've never said yes. She thought Albert was a mean, no good sponge, and Albert was going to have to wait until Hazel was dead to see a penny of his dad's money."

"But what if Albert made Hazel

sick?" I asked Sara. "Then became the attentive and helpful stepson? Wouldn't that loosen her pocketbook?"

Sara's blue eyes flashed in understanding. "Albert's a dog."

"That would be giving dogs a bad name," Karen said.

"How are you going to prove it?" Sara asked.

"I don't think I can, but I still think he's putting something in the food. Maybe nothing as lethal as arsenic but something to make Hazel feel bad, make her have to lean on him. I want to search his truck. If he's putting something in her food he's probably keeping it handy. Where else but the truck?" Karen looked at us expectantly.

Sara put a hand to each side of her face. "This snoop sister stuff really scares me, and Albert has a terrible temper."

"You don't have to go," I said. "No one would blame you."

"Can I just drive the getaway car again? I'd feel a lot safer in the car with the windows up and the doors locked."

Karen laughed. "As long as you don't forget to unlock the doors if we come running."

"All right. I'll do it." She shook her head. "But if Bruce ever finds out about any of this he'll never let me off the farm again."

"I say we go now," Karen said.

Sara was shocked. "Right now? In broad daylight?"

"Do you know where he is?" I asked.

"When Hazel and I were having coffee with Jean Ann this morning, Jean Ann said she and Albert were going to the casino."

"That's a half hour drive. What if the truck's locked?" I asked.

"Oh, I'm sure it will be, but it's not a problem." Karen pulled a ring of keys from her pocket. "The spare set. I took them off the hook in the kitchen while Jean Ann was in the bathroom."

#

Sara was still whining when we pulled into the Mesquakie Casino parking lot. "It's like Albert has ESP where we're concerned. Every time we spy on him we get into a mess."

"Look for his truck," Karen said.

"You're not paying any attention to me," Sara said.

I patted her shoulder. "Calm down, Sara. Third time's the charm. We'll be all right."

Karen pointed toward a sea of vehicles on the south side of the parking lot. "There's the truck."

"Where?" Sara asked.

"On the edge of the lot. Toward the front."

"I see it," I said. "Are you sure he's inside the casino?"

"They've had plenty of time to get settled in at the slots. I'm sure the *ka-ching, ka-chang* of the machines has them mesmerized by now."

Sara pulled up near Albert's green pickup, put the car in park, and Karen and I jumped out. "Remember," I said to Sara, "park a couple rows directly behind us and keep the motor running. If you see Albert, duck down. We'll hide between cars and work our way to you."

By the time I got to the truck Karen had the doors unlocked. We started going through everything, checking the casino entrance occasionally, in case Albert or Jean Ann showed up. I searched the glove compartment while Karen looked in the center console. I found maps, the truck's owner's manual, plastic ketchup packets and napkins.

"Any luck?" Karen asked.

"Nothing here." I took a minute to check the casino door. No Albert in sight. I started searching under the passenger seat while Karen dug through the pocket in the driver's door.

"What have we here?" she said, holding up a plastic bottle of diet capsules. The same brand Jean Ann is taking."

"Maybe they are Jean Ann's?"

"I don't think so. She keeps hers in the kitchen cupboard and uses a fancy pill box when she wants to take a few with her."

"That creep," I said. "If he's putting the diet capsules in Hazel's food, it's no wonder she's having diarrhea. She had no idea she should be watching fat intake. No wonder she was having accidents. It would account for her weight loss too. Poor Hazel. I'd like to wring Albert's neck."

"What now?" Karen asked. "We can't let him get away with this. But on the other hand, I'd hate to mess things up for Jean Ann. She's so happy now that the bills are paid."

Sometimes I'm so devious, I even surprise myself. I had an idea that would keep Hazel healthy and Jean Ann in the money. "Let's go," I said. "Bring the bottle of diet capsules, and you'd better lock the truck up in case they come back before we do."

"Where we going?"

"To the drug store."

#

I bought some harmless fiber capsules. Sara and Karen helped me empty the diet capsules into a plastic baggie and then refill them with the fiber. When we finished, we went back to the truck and put the Alli bottle back in the driver's door compartment.

#

Karen and I were feeling pretty clever with the solution, and Sara breathed a sigh of relief when she drove us out of the casino parking lot. "Did you wipe your fingerprints off everything?" she asked.

Karen laughed. "Don't be so dramatic. Albert's never going to find out we were here."

"Hazel should be feeling better in a day or two," I said. "I just wish we could make Albert pay for what he's done to her.

"Me too," Karen said. "I'd love to get even with him, but I don't know what I could do that wouldn't affect my sister too."

Sara giggled. "I have the perfect punishment."

Karen and I looked at one another in surprise. "Tell us."

"My brother Dan didn't get his size until he was a junior in high-school. When he was a freshman a bunch of guys from the football team were giving him a bad time, so Dan baked Ex-lax into a batch of brownies and put them in the locker room one morning before football practice. By the time noon rolled around several of the bullies had disgraced themselves."

Karen's smile couldn't get any wider. "Talk about sweet justice," she said. "He's my brother-in-law so I'll do the honors. I'll put a batch of brownies in his truck."

"Aren't you worried he'll share them with Jean Ann?" I asked.

"That pig? Share? No way. Trust me, he'll eat every brownie himself. I'll write a note on the computer telling him they're from a secret admirer."

"He'll eat that up," I said. Then, like seventh graders we dissolved into a fit of giggles.

Soon after I got home from the casino I called Kitty's house. No answer. I was relieved. It meant I could stay home and dispense with the bra. It doesn't make any difference what the brand is, and I don't care how many hours it's made to wear, or if it's 'just my size,' after eight to twelve hours in one of those contraptions I'm ready to scream. I wonder if leaner ladies are more comfortable in a bra.

As soon as I'm seventy I'm going to follow my mother-in-law's lead. When she retired, after nearly forty years as a nurse, she decided to let them hang. She quit wearing a bra, except to dressy occasions like weddings or funerals.

It was nearly five o' clock, late enough to consider what to make for dinner. Ruby watched as I washed a few of the potatoes Sara gave me, cut them up, and cooked them in a small pot of water, skins and all. Next I opened a jar of no fat gravy, poured it into a second pot. I shredded a package of lean deli beef, fed a few morsels to Ruby, and added the rest to the gravy.

When the potatoes were ready I mashed them with skimmed milk, salt, pepper, and a nice dab of butter. I ladled a third of the gravy meat mixture over a half cup of potatoes and a slice of Diet Delight bread. Voila! Hot beef sandwich. I added sliced tomatoes to a luncheon-sized plate. Diet experts say a smaller plate tricks you into thinking there's more food. The plate was heaping and I could lick it clean for under five hundred calories, which meant I could have sugarless pudding later.

After dinner I flipped through the television channels. My favorite programs were in summer rerun phase so I didn't find anything that tripped my trigger. The evening was warm but there was a nice breeze. I grabbed a Robert Parker, Jesse Stone novel and a glass of tea and went to the porch.

Usually, by this time of summer the grass is crispy, but we'd had enough rain the lawn was a healthy green and still growing fast. It made me feel a little blue to know another summer was nearly over. The kids would be starting school in a couple weeks. I sighed and opened my book.

I'd been reading for about a half hour when Ryan turned into the drive. He was still in his tan sheriff's uniform. I pulled my sweater around me to hide my floppy boobs and greeted him.

"It's been a long day," he said. He sat in the porch chair next to mine. "Investigating a murder with the state police was stressful, but they're gone now. They headed for Des Moines a few minutes ago."

"That means they think the case is solved and Cindy's guilty," I said.

"I know you're mad at me over Cindy's arrest. That's why I stopped." He sighed.

Exhaustion showed in the slump of

his body, but he went on. "Maggie, it's not that I'm unwilling to keep an open mind. I'm just not sure where to go from here and that heart-shaped button makes her look guilty as hell."

"Cindy did tell you why she was at Kitty's didn't she?"

"Yes, some ridiculous story about a movie on TV and being her own private eye."

"She was telling the truth. I'm the one who told her about the movie."

Ryan stared at me. "She didn't mention it was your idea. Knowing *that* makes her story more believable."

"Well, it was my idea, and I'll testify to that in court. That same movie is the reason I found Grant's body. When I saw a Lexus near Kitty's house, and realized I had the camera in my pocket, I went snooping, but instead of finding Grant in a compromising position with Kitty, I found him dead."

Ryan may have been weary, but there was a glimmer in his eye and his lips curved in a small smile. "I'm not sure a jury will believe that wild story, but you've convinced me. I promise I'll keep digging, Maggie. Something will turn up. Got any more of that iced tea?"

"Sure. Have you had dinner?"

"Not yet."

"I'll fix you up."

Inside I put my bra back on and made up a big plate of beef and potatoes to warm in the microwave. While it was heating I put a tray together with iced tea, silverware and a napkin.

Ryan came to my aid when I got to the screen door. I held Ruby back with my foot while he took the tray.

"This smells fantastic," he said. It's always a treat to get something homemade. I eat most my meals in restaurants."

I settled back in my chair, not bothering to tell him the gravy was from a jar and the beef from the deli. Fresh mashed potatoes from Sara's garden would have to carry the meal. It was fun watching him eat. I hate going to the bother to cook for a persnickety eater.

"Harry was a lucky guy," Ryan said.

"It was more like I was a lucky woman. I fussed at him too much. If I had to do it over I'd give the man a break."

"Ah, you're just a little high strung. Without you, Harry would've been doomed to lead a boring life just like his folks did."

I laughed. "They were boring, weren't they?"

"Do you think you'll marry again, Margaret?"

That question took me by surprise. "Why do you ask?"

"The Alta Grove hotline says you and John Gildenbond are an item."

That made me smile. It'd been a long time since I'd taken a turn in the town's gossip mill. "You mean at my age I can still give them something to talk about?"

Ryan put his napkin on the tray. "You'll be stirring the pot and making things interesting when you're ninety."

"What about you? What happened to your marriage?"

"We were just too different. Neither of us noticed it when we were in college. After we were married and moved to the hired hand's house on the folk's farm, the differences killed us.

Liz was from Chicago, and farming wasn't her idea of living the good life. She hated Alta Grove. Said it was like being in a fishbowl. Everyone knew her business."

"We're used to it," I said. "But to an outsider it must have been like being a butterfly pinned to a board."

"Joey's grown now, but the worst part of being divorced was missing out on so much of my son's life. Seeing your kid every other weekend and a month in the summer doesn't give you much of a chance to be a father."

"Why didn't you marry again? I'm sure there were a dozen Alta Grove women that would've liked living in the country."

"I don't know. Maybe I was gun shy."

"Or maybe you were having too much fun playing the field."

We sat side by side as the sun went down, catching up on all the years between twenty and fifty. It was weird and comfortable at the same time.

Through all my years with Harry I'd
seldom given Ryan a thought. Oh, now
and then a song would come on the car
radio and a wild nerve would zing with a
sudden memory of him, but tonight my
body was in full alert.

Ryan was making a habit of showing
up on my doorstep, and I liked it. I
thought of John and a tad of anxiety
tightened my belly. Was it kosher to be
flirting with two different men?

Settle down, I told myself. *You
aren't married, engaged, or making
promises to anyone. If two handsome men
are interested, relax and enjoy it.*

"As much as I hate to, I have to
go," Ryan said. He flashed that killer
Kryptonite smile. "Dinner was great."

When I stood to say good-bye, Ryan
took my hand and pulled me to him. I
had no choice but to lean against his
chest because my legs were unsteady.
His smell was familiar, stirring
memories that made my breath quicken.

When I looked up I knew I was
asking to be kissed. Ryan's hands
cradled my head and his mouth covered
mine. There was nothing polite in his
kiss. It was full of liquefying heat.
I felt cheated when his mouth left mine.
I wanted to protest. I wanted more.

He kissed my cheek and whispered.
"I have to go."

His words were a slap in the face.
I stepped back from his embrace. It
took everything I had to work up a
smile. "Don't let me keep you." The

words came out with a twinge of
bitterness.

Ryan stopped and turned to me.
"Maggie, my son's driving in from
Chicago. He's probably at the farm
right now. If I stay with you any
longer it's going to take an army to
drag me home."

I smiled bigger. This time it was
genuine. "In that case you can leave
with my blessings."

Ryan shook his head. "You're even
more than I remembered, Maggie.

CHAPTER FOURTEEN

How do you sleep after something like that happens? I slipped between the sheets and replayed the evening. When I got to the kiss, I came within an inch of giving my pillow a passionate work over.

Food.

I needed food to tranquilize me, food to help me sleep. I threw back the bedding. Ruby lifted her head and stared at me through slits of yellow eyes. "Sorry, girl. But I can't sleep." The two of us padded down the stairs to the kitchen and then directly to the refrigerator. It's a wonder there isn't a path worn in the kitchen linoleum.

I pulled out the package of ham, mayo, lettuce, tomato, pickles, onion, and some green pepper for good measure, and built myself a Dagwood sandwich.

Chips, I had to have chips.

For my own protection I don't keep potato chips in the house, but I did have a small bag of multigrain Sun

Chips. If you don't think about it for
too long you can actually convince
yourself Sun Chips are a healthy choice.
Maybe they are for most people, but I'm
half German and half Conehead, which
makes me genetically predisposed to
consumption of mass quantities.

I ate the whole thing and washed it
down with Diet Pepsi. I swear, I can go
to a restaurant, order a double bacon
cheeseburger and fries, but I still want
diet pop.

The worst thing about eating a
midnight snack is: as much as you relish
eating it, when guilt creeps in, and it
always does, it overwhelms all the
pleasure you gained from the food. My
stomach was too full and I was a blob of
remorse. I dropped an Alka-Seltzer
tablet in a glass of cold water, drank
it down with a Tylenol PM, and went back
to bed.

#

The next morning I avoided the
scales. My plan was to be really good.
No sugar, low fat, low calorie. If I
had a good day it would erase last
night's mini binge. I started strong
with oatmeal and a small glass of orange
juice.

After I cleared the breakfast
dishes I made a mug of tea in the
microwave and sat back down at the table
with last night's Waterloo Courier
spread before me. I skimmed the news on
my way to the crossword puzzle.

On the bottom half of the second

page the name, Delmar Crowley, jumped out at me. Delmar was Alice Crowley's husband. He'd left Alice and moved to Waterloo the minute the embezzlement charges were filed against her. Most people didn't blame him, but I know Harry would never have left me; he was no fair weather husband. He would've stood at my side and helped pay restitution.

Delmar had been killed in a mugging while jogging in a park near his apartment complex Wednesday night. He'd been stabbed. The killer took the cash from his billfold, his rings and his watch. There were no witnesses. *Good luck to the police on this one,* I thought. Chances were they'd never find the killer.

The last time I remembered seeing Del was at a party one of the teachers held the Christmas before Alice was charged with embezzlement. I'd felt sorry for her that night. We all sang carols, but Del had sat apart from the fun. Kitty and her husband had split earlier that fall and Grant had been her date that night.

After we'd all had a few drinks our host put on some dance music, but Del stayed glumly in his chair. Finally, just as Harry asked Alice for a dance, Del insisted they leave. I can't say any of us were sorry to see him go.

Still, to read someone you've known was killed while they were doing something as innocuous as jogging is a shock, especially so soon after Grant's murder. How strange that both men should die a violent death. Then again, Harry was gone too. I remembered that night like it was last week, but three of the men who had attended that Christmas party were dead. Downright depressing.

Time to get off my duff and get something done. I showered and dressed, and then called Cindy and invited her to lunch. Later, I ran the usual errands; the post office, the bank, the library. After my date with Cindy, I made one last stop at the grocery store for the round steak they'd advertised, and picked up a half dozen more items before I got to the meat department.

#

It had rained in the night, and now, at two in the afternoon the air was hot and muggy. Cindy had brought up the subject of Kitty again at lunch, and against my better judgment I'd promised to talk to her. I still had that unpleasant chore to take care of, but first I had to put the meat in the refrigerator.

John was clipping the hedge between our houses when I pulled into the drive. I couldn't help but notice the way the sun glimmered on his white hair, the bulge of his calf muscles, and the width of his shoulders. He heard the car and turned to wave.

I clamored out of the driver's seat with the groceries and an armful of library books. John was there to help.

"I'll take the books," he said,
relieving me of their burden.

John's an old-fashioned guy, the
kind of man who treats a woman like
she's too fragile to carry anything
heavier than a bouquet of flowers. He
made me feel as feminine as a southern
belle, and considering my 'take charge'
energy, that was some accomplishment.

He carried my books to the back
door where Ruby greeted me with a
plaintive mew. John stepped back and I
was reminded of his cat allergy.

"I'll just set the books here on
the stair," he said. "Do you have time
to sit on my back deck for a while?"

"I have one more errand to run, but
I can come for few minutes. I'll put
the groceries away and be right there."

#

John's back deck was roomy enough
for a round white metal table with a big
green and white striped umbrella for
shade, and four metal chairs with
matching green and white padded
cushions. A bag of golf clubs were
propped in a corner against the wooden
railing.

"How was your golf game?" I asked,
climbing the three steps to the deck.

He handed me a glass of tea. "I
didn't play worth a damn, but I enjoyed
the heck out of the morning." A huge
grin spread over his face. "I finally
figured out who Albert Minnert is. The
senior men's golf league played today

and Albert was in my foursome. What a jerk."

I laughed. "Albert's pretty full of himself, but worse, he's a bully."

"This morning he was backing up all that braggadocio with great shots and telling the rest of us how to fix our games. He was insufferable."

"I thought you said you had a good morning."

John rattled the ice in his glass and smiled. "There's a port-a-potty between the fourth and fifth hole. Albert was putting out on the fourth green and suddenly his eyes get big, this strange look comes over his face, and he runs like a bat out of hell for the pot."

I did my best to keep a straight face and nodded to encourage John to go on with the story.

"The rest of us putted out then went to the fifth. We waited and waited to tee off, and finally Albert shows up quiet as a mouse. Some of the guys teased him about his dash for the port-a-pot, asked if he'd been eating beans and all that stuff, but they let it go after a bit. I think we were all relieved the man was giving the rest of us a chance to talk."

Poor Albert. I knew what he'd eaten and it wasn't beans.

"Right after Albert tees off on five, he makes another run for the port-a pot. This time he doesn't come out and the rest of us have played on to the sixth. After a little discussion we decided I should drive the golf cart over to see if Albert was in serious trouble."

"Was he still in the port-a-pot?" I asked, keeping an innocent face.

"No. But I saw him creeping through the wooded area south of the pot and drove over to check on him."

"He was in the woods? That's strange."

"I got off the cart to talk to him, and when I was about four feet away I could smell his problem. Albert had filled his pants and he was trying to get back to his truck without embarrassing himself."

I couldn't hold it back. I burst into laughter and the mirth was contagious. John and I laughed till the tears flowed.

"Did you just leave him standing there?" I asked when I could talk.

"You bet. I was driving my brand new golf cart. I bought it right after I moved here. Damned if I was going to let Albert sit in the seat with that load on. I just pretended there wasn't anything odd about the situation and asked if he was too sick to finish the round. When he said yes, I told him one of us would drop his clubs off at his house, and I left. I don't know what he did when he ran out of trees to hide in."

"He'd have to navigate the parking lot once he got back to the first hole,"

I said. The picture of Albert creeping
between vehicles trying to hide his
poopy drawers sent me into fresh gales
of laughter.

I wiped the tears with the back of
my hand. "That story made my day," I
said.

John watched me, cheek in hand, and
a smile on his face. "I've missed
seeing you the last couple days," he
said.

My heart did a little piddy-patter
at the compliment, but I didn't want to
give him a chance to say more. I set my
glass on the deck table and stood.
"I've had fun too, but I'd better get
back. I promised a friend I'd take care
of something for her this afternoon.
Thanks for the tea."

John stood. "How about lunch
tomorrow? I'll take you to Iowa Falls.
It'll be a nice drive. I hear there's a
restaurant on the Iowa River where you
can sit on a deck overlooking the
water."

"Camp David?

"Yes, that's it. Odd name for a
restaurant isn't it?"

"I guess I never thought about it.
It is a strange name, but the food's
good and the river views beautiful. Let
me see if I can get free. I'll call you
tomorrow morning."

#

Why didn't I just say yes to John?
I asked myself. What was holding me
back? Ryan, plain and simple. It was

that damn Ryan. I stood in front of the phone, feeling like a balloon with a slow leak.

Nothing.

I was so sure I'd come home to a blinking red light on the answering machine. *Was I wrong about last night's kiss?* Maybe Ryan hadn't felt what I did, because if he did, he couldn't have let the day go by without calling.

Ruby rubbed against my legs. I scooped her up and held her fresh-smelling fur to my cheek. "Men," I told her, "are a pain in the butt."

#

Kitty works in the office so I felt free to call the school. She wasn't thrilled with the idea of meeting with me, so once she agreed I let her say when and where. She said there was someone she had to see right after work, but it wouldn't take long, and I should come to her house at four-thirty.

I asked myself why I'd given in to Cindy's request to ask Kitty if she and Grant were having an affair. Was it because I felt sorry for her because she was facing a murder trial? Or was it because I was a nosey old broad? I decided it was both.

#

I walked to Kitty's. I needed the exercise, and time to think. I didn't want this encounter to be a rerun of the gym confrontation. I hadn't handled that well. My acrimonious feelings toward Kitty had come to the surface and put her on the defensive, and that was no way to get information.

I was going to have to suck up, apologize, and pretend I was sympathetic to her viewpoint. This would be a challenge, because I wasn't good at any of those things.

When I reached Kitty's house I nearly kept walking, then I thought of Cindy, squared my shoulders, and headed toward the door. From the stoop the house seemed deathly quiet, and then I noticed the front door was half open so I rang the bell. No answer. I eased the door wider and called out to Kitty. Still no answer, so I stepped inside. "Kitty," I called louder, "are you home?"

The air conditioner was working overtime, probably because the door had been left open, and the house smelled wonderful.

Fresh baked peanut butter cookies.

The front room was decorated in discount store 'Palace of Versailles:' blue walls, French tables painted off-white and trimmed in crackled gold, elaborate knick-knacks and cheap prints framed in ornate gold-colored frames. Totally tasteless, except for a stunning carved walnut armoire.

I'm no expert when it comes to antiques, but I thought the armoire was French, not the spindly stuff, but a sturdy Country French style. It had to be nearly eight feet tall because it barely fit under the ceiling.

The room was 'L' shaped and the short end of the 'L' was a dining room with the same blue walls, the same tacky accouterments, and another fantastic piece of furniture, a low cabinet. The beauty of the piece drew me into the room. For the first time I understood all the fuss over patina. I was sure this cabinet had never been refinished. Again, it looked Country French and the walnut was ornately carved.

There were business cards tossed in a cheap pressed glass dish sitting on the dining room table. I sorted through them: Perfect Lawn Care, State Farm Insurance, Holt Brothers Antiques, Jeffery Butts proprietor. Butts? I'd change my name.

An oven buzzer sounded in the kitchen and I swear, I felt so guilty about being in Kitty's house I nearly panicked. When my heartbeat came down to normal I called out cautiously. "Kitty? Are you in the kitchen?"

No answer. She couldn't be far if she had something baking in the oven. She must have run to the store. I decided to get out of the house before she came in from whatever errand she was running and found me snooping.

Kitty had obviously left by the front door, so she'd probably return the same way. There'd be less chance she'd see me if I went out the back. I could walk around the block to give her a chance to get home, then ring the doorbell again.

I didn't make it to the back door.
Kitty's body blocked my path. She was
sprawled on the kitchen floor, her mouth
agape, and a large puddle of dark blood
spread from under her shoulder. A plate
of cookies sat on the table and a mixing
bowl was soaking in the sink. She'd
died while baking cookies. Funny, I'd
never thought of Kitty as the 'Susie
homemaker' type.

Just in case, I checked her wrist
for a pulse. Nothing. I felt like
Nancy Kerrigan. *Why me? Why me?* Why
did I have to be the one to find her
body?

I found a couple pot holders and
took the pan of cookies from the oven.
They were a little brown around the
edges, but they'd be alright.

Heavens! What was wrong with me?
Kitty's body was lying just a few feet
away and I was worried about the cookies
burning. Turning away so I didn't have
to look at Kitty's body, I used my cell
phone to call 911, then sat down at the
kitchen table to wait for Ryan.

I tried, but couldn't ignore the
plate of cookies. Would it be
considered messing with evidence if I
ate one? Who would know? I reached for
the first cookie.

CHAPTER FIFTEEN

I heard the car pull into Kitty's drive and wiped the crumbs from my chin. Ryan was first to arrive. His mouth was tight, and he had a hard look in his eyes. With barely a nod to me he went straight to the body.

Was he mad at me? Maybe he'd noticed the cookie crumbs. He spent a grimly silent minute looking at Kitty's body, then stood.

"Maggie, what in God's green earth brought you to Kitty's house today?"

Before I could form an answer the room began to fill up with people: Deputy Chuck Benninga, Tom Allen, who was Alta Grove's Chief of Police, and Doctor Cummings, the county coroner, arrived one on top of the other.

Ryan spoke to Chuck. "Take Margaret to the living room, get her statement, then take her home."

I'd been dismissed and I was feeling a little huffy about it. I'd

wanted to tell him about Delmar being
killed in Waterloo. *To heck with him*, I
thought. I'd check it out myself.

#

Sara and Karen came over as soon as
they'd fed their families.

"I could use a drink," Karen said.

I got the glasses and rum. Sara got
the ice, diet cola, and lime from the
refrigerator. Karen mixed the drinks,
passed them around, and took a deep
swallow.

"I have to tell you guys about
something I did," Karen said. She took
a deep breath, then exhaled. "Something
I wish I hadn't done."

Sara's eyes widened, "Something
you're ashamed of? What is it?"

"The note I put with the ex-lax
brownies I made for Albert. I told you
Kitty was the woman Albert had the
affair with. She broke it off after she
found out Hazel got all the money when
Albert's dad died."

Karen hesitated, and gave us a
sickly smile. "I wanted to be sure he
ate the brownies," she said.

She stopped talking and I filled in
the rest. "You signed Kitty's name."

"Yes."

Sara's hands flew to her chest and
she started rocking back and forth
chanting, "Jesus, Mary and Joseph,
Jesus, Mary and Joseph. Now Kitty's
dead. We've killed her!"

"Get a grip," I said. "We didn't
kill anyone."

"Oh, but we're responsible."

"We don't know who killed Kitty," I said.

Karen took another long drink. "Albert does have a terrible temper. Everyone's talking about him crapping his pants at the golf course. If he thought Kitty was responsible he might have been angry enough to kill her."

Sara stopped rocking and paced the kitchen. When she got to the refrigerator she spun around to face us. "At the very least we'd be accessories before the fact."

I was exasperated. "Stop it, you two. We didn't kill anyone," I said firmly. "All we did was give Albert the runs. If it turns out Albert killed Kitty it probably isn't because he pooped his pants. Let's give Ryan a chance to find out what happened."

"I can't wait for the cops," Karen said. "My sister's married to that crazy man. I'm worried she'll be next."

"Maybe if we talk to Albert we can figure out where he was this afternoon," I said.

Sara's big green eyes grew bigger. "I'm beginning to think you're as crazy as Albert, Margaret. We can't be running around town playing Charlie's Angels."

Karen and I instinctively turned our backs to one another and crouched. In Angel style we used one hand to form a gun pointing toward the ceiling while the other hand clasps the wrist to steady the aim.

Sara burst into laughter. "I must be a lunatic too." She stepped between me and Karen and pointed her finger gun at the imaginary danger.

#

Jean Ann and Albert usually ate dinner with Hazel on Friday nights. We decided to do a drive-by to see if they were there. They were.

"This is what I'm thinking," I said. "Peanut butter cookies need around twelve minutes in the oven. The oven buzzer went off after I'd been inside Kitty's for say, two minutes max, so Kitty couldn't have been dead for more than ten minutes when I found her."

"Holy crap," Karen said. "You could've walked in on the murderer. You are one lucky woman."

"Funny, I don't feel lucky, "I said with more than a touch of sarcasm. "Kitty's body is the second I've stumbled over in less than a week."

Sara shivered. "I can't stand to think of it."

Neither could I. I hurried on with my thoughts. "We know within a few minutes when the murder occurred, so all we have to do is find out where Albert was at four-thirty this afternoon. Karen should be able to find out by asking Jean Ann a few casual questions."

Karen said, "I think we should go to my sister's house and wait. Albert and Jean Ann will be leaving Hazel's any time now." She checked her watch.

"It's after eight and Hazel goes to bed early. Sara can drive. We'll go to my sister's and park nearby. When we see Albert's truck coming, Sara can drive by casually. I'll wave to Jean Ann, then we can stop like I just thought of something I need to talk to her about."

"You could ask her to go shopping tomorrow," I said.

"That's good," Karen said. "We were just talking about needing jeans."

#

We parked several houses down from Albert and Jean Ann's. Our eyes were focused on the road, waiting for Albert's truck to roll down the street.

"I'm not going to talk to him," Sara said. "And I'm not getting out of this car. I want a ton or more of this car about me if Albert comes unglued."

"Don't worry," Karen said from the backseat. "I'm doing the talking."

"You're not getting out of this car alone," I said. "I'm coming with you."

"Oh fine," Sara said. "I'm the coward."

I put a hand on her shoulder to soothe her. "Don't worry about it. You're the best getaway driver in these parts. We're counting on you to get us out of here if Albert gets nasty."

"Get ready," Karen said. "Here they come now."

Sara paced the van so we'd arrive at Albert's just after they drove into the drive. Karen called to her sister, and then got out of the car with me right behind her.

"Hi Sis. What's going on? Did you eat at Hazel's tonight?"

I said hello to Jean Ann and nodded toward Albert. This was the first time I'd seen him since he'd squeezed my face and he didn't look happy to have me in his driveway.

"What are you guys doing out?" Jean Ann asked pleasantly.

Albert stepped closer to me. "What *are* you doing here?" he asked unpleasantly.

When Jean Ann heard the edge to his voice her face tightened. Karen put a comforting arm around her waist and smiled at Albert. "I wanted to ask Jean Ann if she'd go shopping for new jeans tomorrow morning."

"I don't think so," Jean Ann said. "Me and Albert shopped this afternoon. We got back just in time to get to Hazel's for dinner."

Albert turned to me. "Why don't you go shopping with Karen? You're probably out of brownie mix."

So much for Albert suspecting Kitty of doctoring his sweets. He had me targeted for that crime. "I'm afraid I'm not much of a baker," I said. "When I want sweets I buy them at the grocery store."

Albert raised an eyebrow and sneered at me. "You look like you bought out the whole bakery."

I was angry. But I made my voice as sweet as a kindergarten teacher's.

"You, on the other hand, look like you've lost several pounds. I hope you're not anorexic or using something as harsh as laxatives."

Albert lunged. Karen and Jean Ann tried to hold him back but his face was just inches from mine.

"Don't you dare touch me," I spat at him. "Or maybe I'll tell Hazel about the additives in her food. I bet she'd be much less grateful for your recent attentions to her."

Albert's face paled. I actually saw fear in his eyes.

"What's going on?" Jean Ann asked.

"It's nothing," Karen said. "As usual, Albert is in a foul mood." She turned to her brother-in-law. "Apologize to your wife for making a scene."

Albert looked around, trying to find a way out, but Karen stood determined.

"Sorry, Jean Ann."

Jean Ann beamed. "That's alright, honey. It's so sweet of you to apologize."

#

When I got home I popped the top on a can of Diet Pepsi and flopped into Harry's recliner. What a day. I took a deep drink of the soda and enjoyed the cold burn. I try to drink more water now, but back in the day I'd drink at least four sixteen ounce bottles of regular, full sugar, soda pop. That's one thousand, five hundred and two grams

189

of sugar.

At two hundred calories per sixteen ounce bottle we're talking fifty-six hundred calories a week.

When I switched to diet pop, I was sure I'd drop a ton of weight. Didn't happen, I never lost an ounce. But now I prefer the diet stuff. On top of everything else, I'm probably addicted to aspartame.

I considered what we'd learned this evening. It looked like I could forget about Albert being a murderer. He'd been shopping with Jean Ann when Kitty had been killed. I also realized I'd never actually thought he was guilty. I just disliked Albert enough that if Alta Grove were to be harboring a killer I wanted it to be him.

My mind jumped to Ryan. I'd been trying not to think of him, or his lips on mine, but he kept sneaking into my thoughts, and every time the phone rang I hoped it would be him.

It bothered me when he'd asked Chuck to take my statement instead of talking to me himself. Maybe it was because Kitty's murder demanded his attention, or maybe it was because he didn't want to talk to me. I thought about it for a while and decided, as the younger people say, he just wasn't that into me.

He certainly hadn't been pleased to see me at Kitty's. I wasn't thrilled to find a second body either, but it was hardly my fault. Then I had a flash.

Cindy! Where was she this afternoon? If she was with her sister or someplace where people could vouch for her, Ryan would have to think twice about the murder charge. I went to the phone and dialed.

"Where were you around four-thirty?" I asked without preamble.

"Watching *The View*."

"Was your sister with you?"

"No such luck. She had to go to a teaching seminar."

"Rats. I was hoping you were grocery shopping and had a hundred witnesses."

Her voice was listless. "My luck hasn't been that good lately."

"Has Ryan been there?"

"Yes," she said with a sigh. "He just left. He told me about Kitty and questioned me for a half hour before reminding me not to leave town. Now I don't know what to think. I was sure Kitty was the killer. With her death, it looks even worse for me. Did you ever get a chance to talk to her?"

"I wish I could ease your mind, but that's how I found the body. I was going to talk to her, but she was dead when I got there."

"I guess I'll never know what was going on between them. I want to give Grant the benefit of the doubt, but it's hard." There was a pause, and then Cindy spoke quickly. "I'm so sorry, Margaret. I'm only thinking of myself when I was the one who put you in that terrible situation. Finding Kitty must have been terrible."

"We have to find a way to clear you, Cindy. Someone hated Grant enough to kill him. Surely you have some idea of who it could be."

"No. I've been looking through Grant's things, searching for a clue." She hesitated. "I did found something interesting."

"What was it?"

"A business card from an antique buyer. Grant wrote a number on the back of the card. I checked it against the number he had for Kitty in his cell phone. It's the same."

"That is interesting. I was thinking about the antique pieces I'd seen at Kitty's. "Who's the dealer?"

"Jeffery Butts. His shop is in Des Moines."

I was excited. Maybe Cindy had stumbled on to something. "Did Grant know anything about antiques?" I asked.

"His parents invested in antique furniture so he had some knowledge, but he wasn't an expert."

"Maybe Grant was telling the truth when he said he wasn't having an affair." I told her about the furniture at Kitty's. "Could Grant have been helping her sell them?"

Cindy wasn't buying it. "If that's all it was, why didn't he just tell me?"

"He might have worried it would upset you since they'd once been an item."

"I'd like to believe that. Then I'd at least have something to hang on to."

#

As soon as we said good-bye, I started thinking about a trip to Des Moines. Butts is a name that sticks in your brain. It was the name on the card I'd seen at Kitty's. I decided to do a little antique shopping in Des Moines. If Grant was simply helping Kitty sell her antiques, then Cindy could believe her husband had loved her, and she needed all the comfort she could find.

At eleven-thirty the next morning I was cleaning the kitchen, still wearing my pajamas, the pair with big African animals. I pushed the zebras, printed on the sleeves, over my elbows and rinsed the sponge in soapy water. Ruby hopped on the cupboard and inspected the suds. She swiped her pink padded paw through the bubbles and sneezed, sat back with a quizzical look, then left the room.

I finished washing the appliances and started on the cupboard doors, scrubbing at the dried drips of tea and food juices. The phone rang. I tossed the sponge in the sink and went to answer.

It was John, asking if we could go to Iowa Falls for lunch. I'd forgotten to call him. *Damn that Ryan anyway*, I thought. I said, "I'll be ready at noon."

#

SANDRA NOBLE

It was nearly one o'clock when we got to Iowa Falls. The lunch crowd was thinning so we didn't have a problem being seated on the deck. The river was high, the sky was blue, the clouds fluffy. You could almost smell the sunshine.

A family: mom, dad and three youngsters, passed our table on their way out, leaving only the bus boy, who was filling a gray tub with dirty dishes.

"Looks like we'll have the deck to ourselves," I said.

A pretty, top-heavy waitress, whose nametag read Jennifer, brought the drinks we'd ordered, tall glasses of iced tea with wedges of lemon. She spieled off the specials, then took a pad from her pocket to record our orders. All my promises to make up for last night's calorie splurge went by the wayside. "I'll have the catfish, French fries, and ranch dressing on my salad."

She scribbled on the pad without comment, then looked to John. She seemed considerably more interested in his order.

He closed the menu. "Give me the grilled chicken sandwich on rye, and some cottage cheese with peaches."

He smiled as he handed Jennifer our menus. She smiled back, a touch more friendly than seemed polite, considering I could have been his wife or girlfriend.

"It won't be long," she said to

John, without giving me so much as a glance. "Anything else I can get for you while you wait?"

"No, we have everything we need," he answered.

John was comfortable with her attention. It was obvious he was used to being admired by the opposite sex, leaving me to wonder why such a man hadn't been grabbed up. "Have you ever been married?" I asked.

He grinned. "Where did that come from?"

"I was just noticing how taken our waitress was with you and thinking what a handsome man you are." John's eyes twinkled. "You were gainfully employed," I added.

"Yes?"

"As far as I can tell, you're not a drunk or a drug addict."

John's smile widened. "I live a clean life."

"It seems to me," I said, "the women would be panting for you."

"Are you panting for me, Margaret?"

I started laughing. "I have the first question on the table. Have you ever been married?"

"Yes. I was married ages ago for nearly five years."

"Do you have children?"

"No, my wife didn't want kids. She didn't want the responsibility. Audrey was, well, self-absorbed."

I concentrated on unwrapping the napkin from my silverware, and said,

"I'm surprised you'd be interested in such a shallow woman."

John chuckled. "I was very young when I met Audrey. Young enough I couldn't see beyond her looks. Besides, Audrey loved a good time; there was always an excitement about her. She had a bevy of admirers and I felt like a man among men when she agreed to marry me."

The waitress reappeared with a large tray and dispersed our food. She batted her eyes and nearly dropped a curtsy for John. "Remember, my name's Jennifer. Just holler if there's anything else I can do you."

"This looks perfect." He looked at me. "Doesn't it … sweetheart?"

Jennifer looked at me like it was the first time she'd actually noticed John had company. I watched her smile fade. She gave me a nod and walked away.

I said, "I think the quality of our service is about to take a nosedive … sweetheart."

"Just trying to set her straight."

#

Outside, the catfish's cornmeal breading was fried golden crisp. Inside, its moist white meat was steaming. It was well after one and I was hungry. We took a break from conversation to appreciate the food. Eventually I felt John's eyes on me. I checked my blouse. No food globs. I wiped my mouth in case I had something hung up on my lip. He was still watching. "What?"

"I like looking at you. You're pretty. You're animated. And I like the way the pink in your blouse brings out the rose in your cheeks."

I felt my cheeks grow hot and probably rosier.

"I also like the looks of your catfish. Can I have a bite?"

"So that's what all those compliments were about, catfish." I cut off a nice hunk and put it on John's plate.

"And you're generous. That's probably one of the reasons you were happy in your marriage."

"You weren't happy in yours?"

John gave me a rueful smile. "No."

"Tell me about it."

"There isn't a lot to tell. Audrey married me, but she didn't forsake all others. Eventually I grew up, got a backbone, and threw her out."

"Where is she now?"

"About six months after we divorced she was killed in a car accident."

I put my fork down. "How awful for you."

"That was years ago. Time's eased all those unhappy memories." He reached for my hand. "I haven't stayed single because I'm bitter over my marriage. My mother developed a lot of health issues, and since my sister lived out of state, she moved in with me. She died this past fall. Between work and mom's needs I didn't have time to meet anyone."

I smiled and eased my hand from his at the same time. What in the hell was going on? My fairy godmother had yet to wave her magic wand to make forty pounds disappear and I hadn't been to see the gypsy with the gold-capped tooth either. Time for a change of subject. Besides men, murder was the only thing on my mind.

"I suppose you heard I found a second body?"

"Yes. You'd better be careful or the sheriff will be suspecting you."

"I'd have to have a motive wouldn't I?"

"I'm not sure serial killers need a motive. Maybe they kill for the thrill."

"Not this killer. Grant was found in Kitty's yard, and now Kitty's dead too. There's a connection all right."

"Is your friend Cindy still the prime suspect?"

"I'm afraid so. She was alone watching TV when Kitty was killed, so she doesn't have an alibi."

"I'm sorry to hear that. As far as I'm concerned, unless she's stupid, the fact she doesn't have an alibi makes her innocent. Certainly she wouldn't kill a second time without having an alibi set up."

"Are you sorry you moved to Alta Grove?" I asked. "I'm sure you were expecting small town peace and a low crime rate; instead you found murder and mayhem."

He leaned toward me. In a soft voice he said, "I also got you as a neighbor. I think that's worth the disappointing crime rate."

#

Lunch with John left me with a lot to think about. Life was getting complicated. Since Harry's death I'd been celibate and had taken for granted that was the way it would be from here on out. It wasn't any sacrifice on my part. My body had shut down.

Sometime during the past week the switch had been thrown and I'd come back to life. I realized I missed having a man in my life. I enjoyed lunch with John. I liked a man's attentions. And I was still interested in sex.

John seemed to want more than a romp in the hay. He was willing to wine and dine me. He wanted a relationship that probably included marriage. Marriage was the rub. I'm pretty sure Harry was the only man I could stand living with under my same roof.

On the other hand, Ryan took me nowhere and bought me nothing. All he had to do was drop in and I fell all over myself offering food and yes, face it, anything else he wanted. I had to stop that.

Ryan wasn't thinking about marriage. The danger there was heartbreak. He'd been playing the field for twenty years. There was no reason to think he was going to settle for just one lover for the rest of his life, and

I couldn't see myself going from man to man through the years.

I admonished myself for making a big deal over all this, because John hadn't proposed marriage, and one kiss with Ryan didn't mean he wanted to sleep with me. He hadn't even called since the kiss.

Being single was a lot more difficult than marriage. Too bad I'd taken the ease of living with Harry for granted.

CHAPTER SIXTEEN

My meeting with Jeffery Butts was set for nine o' clock. It was nearly a two hour trip to Des Moines so I had plenty of time to think. Two murders and no one knew why, let alone who the killer was.

I'd wasted a lot of time concentrating on Kitty. She and Grant had certainly renewed a relationship. The phone calls between them proved that. But maybe I'd gone wrong when I'd assumed it was a romantic entanglement. Now that Kitty was dead, all my theories were blasted out of the water.

As for Albert, I'd been trying to fit that square peg in a round hole for days and it wasn't working. He was a nutcase, but not a killer. If he were going to kill anyone you'd think he'd do Hazel in, but he didn't. He made her sick so she'd depend on him and loosen the purse strings, but he didn't kill her.

I kept going back to the Waterloo
Courier article about Delmar Crowley's
mugging. The poor man had been stabbed,
just like Grant and Kitty. Stabbing is
a very personal way to kill. You have
to get in close. Did the killer want
his victims to see who was ending their
lives, or did he just want the
satisfaction of seeing them die, up
close and personal? In less than a week
Del, Kitty and Grant had all been
murdered. What are the odds? There had
to be a commonality.

We'd all known one another back in
the day. We were all connected with the
school. Delmar's wife, Alice, had
worked in the office. When Alice
embezzled the school's money Grant
defended her. Grant was dating Kitty at
the time, and Kitty worked in the office
with Alice.

If I took this a step farther I
could easily expand the list of people.
Cindy came to teach at the school and
Grant married Cindy. For that matter
I'd taught at the same school. Did this
mean Cindy and I were in danger?

Still, if you were playing 'one of
these things doesn't belong' I'd have to
say Delmar was the odd piece of the
puzzle. Alice was the only thing that
tied him to the rest of us. I wondered
where she was.

She'd been on parole. Surely she
had to check in with someone in law
enforcement so there must be a record of
where she went. I made a mental note to

ask Ryan about it as I parked in the lot attached to Holt Bros. Antiques.

#

I like antiquing with the girls. I shop for Florentine, my Depression glass pattern, old Christmas decorations, and bits and pieces that suit my Victorian house. The shops we frequent are Daze of the Past, or Aunty Q's. Part of the fun is digging through overcrowded shelves to discover a treasure, like the red wooden-handled potato masher that hangs on my kitchen wall.

When I stepped into Holt Brother's Antiques, I immediately understood the difference between collectables and true antiques. The very air of the shop smelled expensive.

Jeffery Butts came from somewhere in the middle of the shop to greet me. "Mrs. O'Brian?"

"Yes." I offered my hand. "Nice to meet you, Jeffery."

Jeffery Butts was a tall, very lean man in his thirties. The dark silk ascot fluffed at his throat accentuated his sad brown eyes. He took my hand and smiled with thin lips set in a long skeleton-like face. If he'd been a defendant in a murder trial every woman on the jury would have voted guilty on appearances alone.

"You said you were a friend of Grant Waveland?" His voice was gravelly, like a man who'd smoked for too many years.

"Actually, his wife, Cindy, is my

friend."

He nodded. "I heard about Grant's
murder of course, so I'm curious as to
why you're here. We can talk in my
office."

"I was hoping you could shed some
light on why anyone would want to kill
Grant," I said, when I was settled
across the desk from him.

Jeff arched an eyebrow. "You're
making me more curious. I love
thrillers and mysteries, especially
Agatha Christie. Now a younger, and
much more attractive, Miss Marple has
come to question me."

I grinned. Miss Marple. I liked
that. In fact, despite Jeffery's rather
sinister appearance, I was beginning to
like him. "Tell me about Grant."

Jeffery leaned toward me. "I don't
usually indulge in gossip with
strangers. Maybe you'd better tell me
why you're so interested in this
murder?"

It seemed Jeffery had a curiosity
that matched my own. I studied his face
for a moment, then decided it couldn't
hurt to tell him. "I'm sure you read in
the papers that Grant's wife has been
arrested for his murder. I believe
she's innocent."

He leaned back again with his long
thin fingers posed in a church steeple.
"What else?"

"What do you mean?" I sat back in
the chair eying him. "Isn't saving an
innocent woman from prison enough?"

"Of course it is." Jeffery's sad
brown eyes glittered with humor. "I
just wondered why the sheriff isn't here
asking questions rather than a very
pretty Miss Marple."

That dog. He knew I was holding
back. I laughed. If a little honesty
would get me what I wanted, so be it.
"There is one more, rather embarrassing,
little thing." I took a breath, then
rushed in. "I have feelings for the
sheriff. I'm not sure how deep they
run, but he's hurt my feelings and I'd
love to solve this murder, or at least
uncover the clue that unravels it."

Jeffery pursed his lips to one
side, thinking about what I'd said.
"I'll tell you what I know about Grant.
He was a little too serious for my
taste. He was always ambitious, so he
worked at making friends in high places.
Not everyone liked him, but he wasn't so
disagreeable you'd want to kill him."

"Then you and Grant weren't close
friends?"

Jeffery smiled. "No. Grant was a
good guy, almost too good."

"A man can be too good? I haven't
met one of those."

Jeffery chuckled and leaned back
comfortably in his chair. "We were a
bunch of high spirited fraternity boys,
into pranks and beer parties. Grant was
dedicated to the rules. For instance, a
bunch of us would get together in the TV
room to watch Seinfeld. We weren't
supposed to drink in the house on

weeknights, but a couple of the guys would pop a beer. No big deal. Grant walks in, looks around, sees the beer, and announces that if the alcohol isn't dumped immediately he'll be forced to turn us in."

"He doesn't sound like the kind of guy who'd cheat on his wife."

Jeffery tilted his head and thought about it. "Sex is different," he said. "Even preachers and priests are tempted when it comes to sex. It is hard to see Grant as a cheating husband, but where women are concerned, you never know."

"Did he talk about women with you?"

"No. We were in the same frat house, which was reason enough he could expect my help with anything in the antique field, but we didn't exchange confidences."

"How did he know you're in the antique business?"

"The original Holt brothers were my mother's father and my great uncle. I grew up in the business and always knew I'd take over the shop one day."

"Was Grant interested in antiques too?"

"I believe his parents were more interested. Grant had picked up a fair amount of information by osmosis. Like a lot of people, the Waveland's use antiques as an investment. They get to live with beautiful things, and at the same time their money grows along with the value of the antique."

"Then Grant was one of your

customers?"

"Occasionally. The last time I saw him he brought me photos of a large French commode and an eighteenth century armoire, beautiful pieces. He wanted to know their value."

My heart skipped a beat. I was sure Jeffery was describing the antiques I'd seen at Kitty's. "What were they worth?"

"Maybe thirty-five for the commode and nineteen or twenty for the armoire."

I swallowed. "Thousand?"

He grinned and said, "Yes."

"Did he want you to sell them?"

"He didn't say. He seemed anxious to keep everything low key so I didn't ask questions, but he would've known I'm in contact with people interested in quality pieces." He handed me his business card. "You can pass this on to Grant's family if they're interested in selling."

"I'm sorry. The furniture isn't theirs and I think the owner's lost interest in the sale."

Jeffery's face reflected his disappointment. "Too bad, it would have been a nice commission."

Satisfied I'd learned what Jeffery knew about Kitty's antiques, I thanked him for his time and started home. I puzzled over why Grant would travel all the way to Des Moines to ask the value of Kitty's furniture.

Jeffery didn't make Grant sound like a guy who'd indulge in an affair, but he was certainly in Kitty's house for some reason or he wouldn't have known about the antiques, and he'd even taken pictures of them. Did Kitty know that?

Even I knew the commode and armoire at Kitty's place were special. With Grant's knowledge, he must have been astounded that Kitty had such pristine pieces. If he owned a small digital camera or used his cell phone he could've taken the photos without her knowledge, but why was he suspicious of her? What did he think she'd done?

If I could find the answer to those questions I'd probably know why Grant, Kitty and Delmar, were dead. I just had to be careful that I didn't end up alongside them.

CHAPTER SEVENTEEN

I was back in Alta Grove by one o'
clock and hungry. Sleuthing had given
me an appetite, but first things first.
I needed to call Ryan. After my talk
with Jeffery I realized holding out on
him was childish. Compared to three
murders, the crime of brushing me off
wasn't worth consideration.

I gave myself a good talking to
before punching out the number. I
wanted to be cool, businesslike, when I
talked to Ryan. I sure didn't want him
to think I had given the kiss on my
front porch any more thought than he
had. I'd already given the man my
virginity. Wasn't that enough?

Okay, maybe I was being a little
melodramatic. It wasn't as though Ryan
had to seduce me. I'd been just as
anxious to experience sex as he'd been
to give me the experience.

Maybe a relationship with Ryan was
out of the question, but at the very

least, the man owed me a meal.

"Did you read about Del Crowley in the paper?" I asked, when we were connected.
"I haven't exactly had time to read the papers, Maggie. Who's Del Crowley?"
"Alice Crowley's husband, surely you remember Alice."
I could almost hear him thinking. "Oh yeah," he said, "the woman who embezzled all that money from the school?"
"Del was her husband."
"Right. I remember now."
"Then you don't know Del was killed?"
"How'd he die?"
"The Waterloo Courier said he was bashed in the head, stabbed in the back, and robbed. At the time I didn't associate his death with Grant's, but now that Kitty's dead . . . "
"And she was killed with a knife too," Ryan added.
"Yes. I've got a couple ideas about the murders. If you buy me lunch I'll tell you about them."
"I'll get some chicken from the deli and be at your place in fifteen minutes."

#

Like I've said, I'm not interested in marriage. But I still wanted Ryan to think of me as a desirable woman. I didn't want him to think of me as one of those invisible sexless fifty year olds

210

that men pass over without a second thought. I brushed my teeth, fixed my hair, and changed into a fresh blouse. The one I'd been wearing had a spot where I'd dribbled the tea I'd bought for the drive home from Des Moines.

I started a pot of coffee, set the dining room table, and then looked around the room. Cozy. I put a CD in the player but decided it was too much; too obvious I was setting a scene. Ruby followed me around like a puppy dog trying to figure out what was happening. "I want you to be on your best behavior, girl, even if Ryan ignores you. You know, some men think it's disloyal to dogs to like a cat."

"Meow," Ruby replied.

#

"Alice Crowley has to be the connection," Ryan said as he set the bucket of chicken on the table.

Talk about stealing my thunder. He pulled up a chair, searched through the chicken and put a golden, crisp thigh on his plate. "Is that coffee I smell?"

"It's in the kitchen." I shouldn't have told Ryan about Del's murder until he got here. I'd wanted to connect Alice to the murders and astound him with my Sherlock Holmes' deductions. He was taking the wind from my sails.

Ryan came back from the kitchen with a steaming cup of coffee. "It's lucky for me you saw the article about Del. What I can't figure out, is what her motive for killing these people would be."

I pulled the delectable crusty skin
from a chicken breast, and with regret
sat it aside. "What did you think of
Kitty's decorating scheme?" I asked.

Ryan looked up from his food. "I
didn't pay much attention." His eyes
got a faraway look. I knew he was
trying to picture Kitty's place. "It
was a little tacky," he said. "But
divorced school secretaries don't have a
lot of spare cash to spend on that
stuff. Why?"

"What would you say if I told you
Kitty had two pieces of antique
furniture worth a total of fifty-five
thousand dollars?"

Ryan pursed his lips and whistled.
After he thought for a moment he said,
"How do you know they're worth that
much?"

"I checked with an antique dealer.
Don't you wonder how she got them?"

"She could have inherited them."
He fished another piece of chicken from
the box.

"Maybe, but her folks are still
alive. If her grandparents had owned
furniture that valuable, don't you think
they'd leave them to their kids rather
than a grandchild?"

"So how do you think she got them?"

I wiped the grease from my mouth
before I spoke. "Maybe Alice Crowley
wasn't guilty of embezzling from the
school. Kitty could have done it. She
couldn't put the cash in the bank, it

would've drawn attention to her if she'd started throwing too much money around."

"So you think she invested most of the cash in antiques."

"Yes. She was dating Grant at the time, and his parents invested in antiques. She could have gotten the idea from him. She bought two great pieces, then decorated her house around them to keep them from standing out. In your case the tactic worked."

Ryan sat back and took a sip of hot coffee to give himself time to process my theory. "Then why did Alice plead guilty?"

"Remember the ring you found in Alice's bedroom?"

"Sure. That's what sealed the arrest. The ring was in her possession. We were able to trace its purchase back to the school's credit card, and she had access to that card."

"Pretty damning evidence, wouldn't you say?"

"I thought so."

"Maybe Grant did too. He was her lawyer. I think he took a look at the evidence and thought the only way Alice could be sure of avoiding jail time was to plead guilty. Alice had a clean record. With a guilty plea she could expect to pay restitution and be paroled. If she decided on a not guilty plea, she'd have to go through a jury trial and take a big chance on going to jail."

"Okay, but why kill Grant? He was

just trying to keep her out of jail."

"Think what Alice's life must have
been like," I said, between nibbles at
the crusty skin on my chicken wing.
"Seventy- thousand dollars for
restitution is a lot of cash to come up
with, especially if you weren't the
embezzler.

After Del divorced her, I bet it
took every cent of her share of equity
in the house and everything else she had
to pay restitution, and don't forget
lawyer's fees. Her reputation was shot.
She had to leave the community she
loved, and she was dead broke."

"And you think she's gone a little
crazy and come back to kill the people
that ruined her life."

I nodded. "That's what I'm
thinking."

Ryan's eyes opened wide. "And like
you said. Grant was stuck on Kitty at
the time."

"Right," I said with a touch of
smugness. Which is why Grant never
considered Kitty as a suspect and there
was no one else to cast doubt on Alice's
guilt."

Ryan bit his bottom lip in thought.
"Kitty had access to all the same tools
for embezzlement."

"If I were Alice," I said, "and had
several years to consider the injustice
done to me, I might blame my lawyer for
not searching out every avenue of
defense. People in Alta Grove seldom
lock their door unless they're going on

vacation. It would've been easy for Kitty to plant the ring in Alice's bedroom."

Ryan let out a sigh. "I guess it is possible Alice was innocent. After she pleaded guilty I sure as heck didn't look in any other direction."

I thinly buttered a second piece of bread. "The first thing we have to do is to find out where Alice is."

Ryan wiped his hands with his napkin. "No *we* about it, Maggie, that's the first thing *I* have to do. I'll ask Chuck to check with her parole officer. What *you* have to do is stay out of this. You've already discovered two bodies. Isn't that enough excitement for you?"

"I certainly don't want to find any more bodies, but if I hadn't told you about Del Crowley's murder and Kitty's antiques, you'd still be in the dark. I'd like to be involved. Cindy is a friend of mine and I don't want what happened to Alice to happen to her."

"I admit you've been a big help. Now butt out before you get hurt. If Alice is our killer she's probably unbalanced. If you stumble into the wrong place you could be her next victim."

#

As soon as Ryan left I went to Cindy's. "I saw Jeffery Butts, the antique dealer," I told her. "Grant was trying to find the value of some antiques Kitty owned." I glanced at her from my side of the kitchen table.

SANDRA NOBLE

Cindy was doubtful. "If Kitty owned good quality antiques she must have known something about them. Surely, she could've figured out how to sell them without Grant's help."

"I'm not sure Kitty was planning to sell. How long had you suspected Grant was having an affair?"

"At least a month before he was killed."

"And before that Grant seemed happy and your marriage was good?"

"Yes," she said sadly, "then over the past weeks he became distant. He'd always adored Angie, but when Kitty's calls started, he was impatient with her. He lost interest in making love to me." Tears welled up in Cindy's eyes. "It was like he quit loving us overnight."

I went to her and gave her a hug. "I know it's just my opinion, but I think Grant was faithful."

Cindy put her hand to her mouth and closed her eyes. When she regained her composure she said. "You have no idea how much that means to me. I've been so angry with Grant that I haven't even been able to mourn his death."

I patted her back, then went back to my chair. "Whatever Kitty and Grant were involved in, it was much more serious than an affair. Serious enough that someone killed them, and I think it has to do with Alice Crowley."

"Alice? I know Grant was her lawyer when she embezzled money from the

216

school, but that was years ago. Grant
and I weren't even seeing one another
then."

"Maybe I'm crazy, but her ex-
husband was mugged and killed in
Waterloo. I think it's tied up with
what's going on here."

"Del's dead? That is too weird."

"My thought exactly. This is a lot
bigger than affairs and jealous wives
and lovers. Alice hasn't called here
has she?"

"I don't think so. We don't have a
land phone and I checked out every
number recorded in Grant's cell when I
suspected he was seeing Kitty. I didn't
notice anything else out of line."

"What about email? Did you check
that?"

"No. Grant never used our laptop.
He said he spent so much time on the one
in the office that the last thing he
wanted when he got home was to sit in
front of a computer screen. Besides,
the police took it. They took the one
at his office too."

"I guess that's that," I said. "If
there'd been any communication from
Alice, Ryan would have checked it out by
now."

Cindy thought for a moment. "The
police asked if we have a safe and I
opened the one in Grant's office, but I
forgot about the little safe in our
bedroom. It's in the wall behind a
painting. We never use it, but if Grant
were hiding something he might have put

it there.

I followed her to the bedroom, a tailored room with light green walls and purple print curtains with a matching bedspread. Classy.

I was excited about the safe, sure we'd find something to help make sense of Grant and Kitty's murders. Cindy removed a framed landscape scene from the wall. The small recessed safe was open a crack. I squeezed closer when Cindy pulled the door open.

Nothing.

Cindy expelled a breath. Disappointed, we sat on the bed to consider our options. "The police may have found this after all. It wasn't locked so they wouldn't need me to open it."

Can you think of anyplace else they might have missed?" I asked.

Cindy shook her head. "They were pretty efficient."

"Maybe, but they missed Jeffery's business card."

"That was in a suit I'd taken to the cleaners. They always check the pockets before they process the clothes, then return the items they find when you pick up the cleaning. The police never saw it, and I'd forgotten all about it until the dry cleaners called."

Cindy put a finger to her lips and got a surprised look on her face. "There is one place the police may not have checked. In the basement laundry room I have a wastepaper basket I use to empty the lint trap.

"Grant thought littering was a major sin. He stuck everything in his pockets. I'd find all kinds of stuff, like paper clips or gum wrappers. There probably isn't anything important, but we can look."

#

I once read about an artist who used lint from the drier to make pictures. He wanted people to send him their most colorful lint. He didn't want blues and grays because they were easy to come by. He wanted the stuff you get when you wash a colorful sweat shirt or towel for the first time. He wouldn't have been interested in Cindy's lint. No orange, reds, or yellows.

I lifted each fragile blanket of fluff, searching for something Grant might have written on. There was a rubber band, and the spearmint gum wrappers Cindy had mentioned, a plastic pop bottle lid. Cindy was right. Grant was no litterbug. He brought his trash home in his pockets.

The payoff was at the bottom of the bin, a half sheet of paper that had been folded into pocket-sized quarters. Cindy and I sat down on the basement steps to open it.

Was sex with that whore worth sacrificing an innocent person? Did you think because your client didn't go to prison there was no harm?

"Oh my God," Cindy said. Do you think this is from Alice?"

"That would be my guess."

"If she knew Grant the way I did she'd know he'd never throw a client to the wolves for personal gain. He was honest to a fault. I was never brave enough to ask him if I looked fat in an outfit. I'd be afraid of the answer."

I paced the basement floor. Jeffrey Butts and Cindy agreed about Grant's character. He was a stickler for the rules, even when it made him unpopular. Excited thoughts tumbled from my brain and out my mouth. "A note like this might send Grant to Kitty's door to ask questions."

Cindy was excited. "Yes, and Grant had some knowledge of antiques. Once he was inside her house he'd recognize the value of her furniture."

"And wonder how Kitty could afford such exquisite pieces," I added. "After getting this note it wouldn't have taken Grant long to put it all together."

Cindy nodded. "That's why he wasn't himself. Wondering if he'd helped ruin the life of an innocent person would have devastated Grant. If Kitty couldn't convince him she'd come by the furniture honestly he would've wanted to clear Alice's name and get her money back."

"Unfortunately, he didn't get the chance to set things right."

CHAPTER EIGHTEEN

I wanted Trans fats. I wanted high
fructose corn syrup. I wanted them bad.
It's like after you think you've kicked
the cigarette habit, and then, out of
nowhere, an overwhelming intense
physical urge to light up envelops you.

I pulled into Quick Stop and walked
the aisles. *Minimize the damage*, I told
myself. *Just one choice, not a bag full
of goodies.* I looked at the chips. No.
I needed sweets. I checked out the
Little Debbie's and the Hostess Ding
Dongs. Close, but not quite.

In the corner of the store stood a
lighted Crispy Cream donut display. That
was the ticket. I moved to the cabinet
like a bee to a nectar-filled peony and
stood transfixed, staring at the
choices. Glazed, that's what I wanted.
They looked small. Could I hold myself
to just one? I narrowed my eyes,
drawing strength from within, then
quickly pulled a sheet of waxed paper
from its box, opened the clear plastic
door, and took just one glazed donut.

#

I wouldn't be safe from the call of
donuts not chosen until I pulled away
from the store. I fastened the
seatbelt, turned onto Main, and reached
for the donut. My mouth was watering,
nearly overflowing, as the donut neared
my lips.

Heaven.

I closed my eyes for a second,
waiting for the sugar rush to hit. Oh
yeah. Sugar is my drug of choice. I'll
diet for the rest of my life. Unless I
find that genie in the toothpaste tube,
or in a bottle of Diet Pepsi, to grant
me three wishes, I'll never be free from
the call of sugar. The best I can do is
what I did today. Minimize the damage.

#

I slowed when I reached Ryan's
office. I'd planned on giving him
Grant's note on my way home, but when I
saw two state police cars parked in
front of the cop shop I decided against
it. If I showed up with a piece of
evidence Ryan had missed he'd look bad.
The note could wait.

Too wired from sugar to go home, I
thought of Hazel. I hadn't checked on
her since Karen and I'd had the
confrontation with Albert. It was early
enough she wouldn't be cooking supper
yet. I passed my street and drove to
Hazel's cozy ranch house.

She was glad to see me. "Come in,
come in," she trilled. She sat me in a
1970s gold-colored, overstuffed rocker

and went for two glasses of lemonade.

"You look like a million bucks," I told her.

Hazel patted her freshly coiffed hair and smiled. "I feel wonderful. For a while I was afraid I'd lost my good health so I'm grateful. I guess Doctor Hepple was right. I did have the flu."

I couldn't bring myself to fully agree. "Maybe," I said. It was on the tip of my tongue to tell her the truth about her illness, but she didn't give me the chance.

"One good thing about being sick, I learned I could rely on Albert. It's such a good feeling not to be alone in this world. You have a son and a daughter so you wouldn't know how it feels to be without family."

I nodded sympathetically. Hazel was right. Since Harry's death my kids have been wonderful, and I knew they'd come as soon as possible if I needed them. Maybe she was better off not knowing Albert was using her.

"Just between us," Hazel said, "I've been too judgmental about Albert and Jean Ann. It was Albert's dad's money, so why not share it with them now?"

"I can't think of a single reason why not," I said. "Just be sure to safeguard enough that you have everything you need."

"Oh well, at my age I don't need much." Hazel lowered her voice and

smiled. "I'm not stupid. I know Albert
gambles and handles money poorly.
Albert would blow every cent that came
his way. I've set up a trust fund.
Starting next month he'll get a monthly
allowance to insure his future."

"Have you told Albert?"

"Yes. He wasn't thrilled with my
decision, but Jean Ann sees the benefits
of a monthly stipend rather than a lump
sum, and she's convinced Albert it's for
the best."

After we visited a few more
minutes, I finished my lemonade and
Hazel walked me to the door. I promised
I wouldn't be a stranger and said good-
bye, satisfied Hazel would be fine.
Albert no longer had anything to gain by
harming her.

\#

At the end of the drive I stopped
to check the street traffic. Albert's
green truck was headed my way fast. He
screeched to a halt, blocking my exit,
and jumped out of the truck in a flash.
That man moved mighty quickly for a big
ketchup bottle.

"What are you doing here? What
have you been telling her about me?"

"Calm down, Albert. Hazel's at the
window."

He turned toward the house. Hazel
stood in the big front window waving at
him.

"Wave back," I said cheerfully.

Albert plastered a sick grin on his
face and waved.

"I was just checking on Hazel's
health," I said. As long as you're
treating her right you've nothing to
fear from me. As a matter of fact, I'm
impressed, Albert. You've made your
stepmother happy."

"The old bat isn't all that bad,"
he said.

"Why Albert, you have a heart."

He had the grace to be embarrassed.
"I wasn't trying to hurt her. I just
wanted to make her soft on me. I
stopped putting those pills in her food
the day she messed her pants at the
grocery store. I even tried to get rid
of the rest of the food I'd emptied
pills into, but Hazel got upset about me
wasting food so I had to leave it."

I don't know why, maybe because he
looked so hangdog, but I believed him.
"Alright, Albert. Just know I'll be
dropping in on Hazel now and then."

He nodded.

"Now will you move the blasted
truck so I can go home?"

#

I drove past the cop shop again.
The state police were gone but Ryan's
car was in his parking slot. I pulled
in.

He looked up when I walked into his
office. The lines in his face were more
pronounced than I'd noticed before. He
was tired. I wanted to step behind him
and rub his shoulders, but I'd have to
settle for giving him a piece to the
puzzle he was trying to solve.

"Have you located Alice Crowley," I asked.

"Not yet. I spent most the day in Waterloo. I checked with the detectives working on Del Crowley's case. I've questioned the people Del worked with, and some of his friends. I showed everyone a picture of Alice, but so far no one's recognized her."

"What did her parole officer say?"

"Alice asked permission to move to California. She had a job lined up and relatives who agreed to take her in until she was on her feet. No one's heard from her since."

"California's a big state," I said.

"Could be she never even went to California. She never checked in."

I handed him the baggie with the note. "I found this at Cindy's today. I would've given it to you sooner but the state police were here."

"Sit down," he said. He read the note through the plastic bag, looked up at me, and then read it again. "Where'd you find this?"

I told him about the lint basket. I also told him about the card Cindy found in Grant's suit with Kitty's number on it and my meeting with Jeffery Butts. When I finished I said, "I think Alice wrote the note."

"Listen, Maggie, I admit Alice looks good for this, and if you hadn't spotted the Courier article about Del Crowley's death maybe I wouldn't have seen the possibility. But now you have to promise me you'll stop snooping around."

"I'm not doing this for fun, Ryan. I'm trying to keep my friend out of prison. Drop the charges against Cindy and I'll go home and take up knitting."

"Maggie, I'd like to let Cindy off the hook, but try looking at this another way. Who came up with the card leading you to the antique store?"

"Cindy."

"And who thought to look in the lint basket where you just happened to find this note?"

"Cindy. But it wasn't like that Ryan. I'm the one who pushed to look for something that would connect Alice and Grant. There had to be a call or an email or something that would send Grant off to see Kitty after all this time. Besides, Grant did go to the antique store and he did ask about the value of Kitty's antiques."

"I'm not saying Cindy's guilty, but I don't have enough to clear her. To do that I've got to find Alice Crowley."

Maybe I can help find her. I've done a pretty good job so far."

"Go home, Maggie."

I shot him a dirty look, angry to be dismissed like a child after giving him the gift of the clue I'd found.

Ryan stood and came around his desk. "Maggie."

I was too mad to answer, and turned to leave. Ryan took hold of my arm and turned me about. His eyes were narrow.

"Don't do this to me. I have enough to worry about. Three people have been killed, and if you keep digging up information you're going to be a target too."

Deputy Chuck Benninga peeked in the office door. "The Waterloo detective wants to talk to you. Del Crowley's girlfriend found a strange note in his desk."

"I'm staying," I said. "I want to know what that note says."

"If I tell you what the note says, will you leave the investigating to me?"

I crossed my fingers and said, "Yes."

"Line two," Benninga said.

Ryan went back to his chair and picked up the phone. "Sheriff Harrison here."

He wrote down the contents of the note as the Waterloo detective read, then told him about the one I'd found. They discussed the case for a few more minutes and made arrangements to meet for breakfast in Waterloo the next day. After Ryan hung up he pushed the paper across the desk to me.

Does a man who abandons his wife in her darkest moment deserve to find happiness?

I looked up. "Did I hear Chuck say Del had a girlfriend?"

"Yes."

"I guess that really ticked Alice

off." Then a thought struck. "Kitty must have received a note too. Did you find anything at her place?"

"No. I'll send Chuck out to look again, but even if she did get a note it doesn't mean we'll find it. If she threw it away it's in a plastic bag along with thousands of others at the landfill."

#

At ten the next morning I walked the six blocks to the Main Street Coffee House to meet Karen and Sara. Opening the door was like stepping into an aroma therapy session. Amaretto must have been the flavor of the day because it was the underlying scent.

The air hummed with conversation. I returned cheery greetings from friends as I made my way to our table. Hazel's crowd was sharing a belly laugh. I gave her a princess wave as I passed.

"Hazel looks wonderful, doesn't she?" Sara said.

"Yes, I'm feeling much better about her." I took my usual chair, then told them about my run-in with Albert. "Before I left he was actually behaving like a human being."

"And my sister says Albert has promised to stay out of the casinos," Karen said. "They're even planning a vacation in Maine this fall. It's been a long time since Jean Ann's been this happy."

"It'll be better for you too," I said. You won't have to be their personal loan officer."

Karen laughed. "Or listen to all Jean Ann's 'woe is me' phone calls."

We gave our drink orders to Mike, the coffee shop proprietor, and went back to our conversation. Before long I realized Sara was quieter than usual. "What's going on with you, Sara?"

"I'm sorry. I was just thinking about something Mom said."

My ears perked up at the possibility of one of her 'Mom' stories.

"What did the old bat say this time?" Karen asked.

Sara sighed. "She stopped by the house, and I confess, I was eating the Ho Ho's I'd bought for the kid's school lunches, and Mom said they were going to have to call Omar, the tent maker, if I got any fatter."

Karen was right; Sara's Mom was an old bat. She'd gone too far this time. "What does she want? You've lost thirty pounds."

"I know, but I have at least seventy to go and I've been cheating all week. It's discouraging."

Karen shook her head. "No, Sara, losing thirty pounds is a grand accomplishment."

"I didn't lose anything last week."

"Oh Sara," I said. "There are always setbacks. I'd nearly reached my goal weight when Harry died and here I am twenty pounds up. We just hang in there."

Sara spoke to Karen. "If I could

get down to my goal weight like you have, I wouldn't have to worry about it."

Karen nearly spewed a mouth full of coffee. "Is that what you think?" She dabbed her lips with a paper napkin. "You think if you get down to goal its smooth sailing? I may look thin on the outside, but Sara, I'll always be a fat girl. I'm just one emotional disaster from weight gain."

"What do you mean?" Sara asked.

"Fat people are never safe, even when they're skinny. When you're fat you have the emotional struggle to lose the weight. When you're thin, you have the same emotional struggle to keep the weight off."

"So it never gets better?"

"Sure it does," I said. "While you're fighting to eat right and exercise you look great and get to buy cute clothes."

Sara looked sad. "I don't know if I can keep the weight loss going. And even if I do I know I won't win the war. You guys are stronger than me."

I reached across the table and patted her hand. "Sara, from where I sit, you're the one with the strength."

She lowered her voice. "I may as well tell you. I've made an appointment with a doctor in Des Moines. He does bypass surgery."

Karen and I exchanged openmouthed glances. She recovered faster than I did. "That's pretty drastic," she said.

Sara lowered her eyes. "I know. I'm not positive I'm doing it yet."

"You've never mentioned you were considering an operation," I said.

"My best friend in high school, Amy, was another fat girl. We were eating buddies. When I went to our high school reunion earlier this summer I didn't expect to see her. Amy always refused to come because she was embarrassed about her weight. Anyway, she was there and she was beautiful, thin and confident. When I asked her how she'd done it she told me she'd had a bypass."

"I can't say I've never thought about it," Karen said. "I think I was too scared to do it. They say a major operation can take ten years off your life."

I considered the statement. "That's true, but yo-yo dieting and being overweight isn't any better for you."

"Will you kick me out of Fit Girls if I go through with it?" Sara asked.

I laughed. "Absolutely not. Even if you decide on the operation you'll still have to exercise and eat good food to be healthy."

"You're stuck with us," Karen said, "through thick and through thin."

#

A bypass, I thought as I walked home. I'd never been more than fifty pounds beyond a healthy weight. Fat enough to look and feel like crap, but not fat enough that a reputable doctor would operate on me. Wouldn't it be wonderful to put the struggle behind me?

The battle with weight had always been such a huge part of my life. I wondered what it'd be like to wake up in the morning without the first thought of the day being about starting or staying on a diet.

What would I do with all the extra energy and mind space if I weren't always trying to solve the problem of being fat? Maybe I'd write the great American novel, or invent something the world couldn't live without.

Beep, beep!

Lordy! I'd been deep in thought when the horn sounded. Being pulled back to reality felt like a slap in the face.

John leaned from his car window. "I'm sorry, Margaret. I didn't mean to startle you."

My body was still in fight or flight mode, but I made my voice pleasant. "Good Morning, John."

"I'm on my way to the book store in Waterloo. Do you want to ride along?"

I couldn't think of a better way to spend the next few hours. "Sounds like fun." I walked around the car and got in.

SANDRA NOBLE

CHAPTER NINETEEN

At Barnes and Noble I bought the
newest John Sandford thriller to come
out in paperback. Lucas Davenport is
the perfect hero. Tall, well dressed,
rich, and sexy. Sandford is allowing
Lucas to age so I don't feel like a
dirty old woman when I drool a little
over him.

John took me to lunch at Red
Lobster where I indulged in another
favorite, Salmon New Orleans. The
salmon's seasoned with Cajun spices and
topped with a lemon butter sauce with
plenty of little shrimp. Love it.

Again, John was treating me to a
meal. "Was your wife a fat girl, John?"

John laughed. "Audrey was curvy."

I eyed the basket of cheesy
biscuits, but resisted. "Is that a nice
way of saying she was fat?"

He's eyes crinkled as he smiled.
"I certainly never thought of her as
fat, but I've never been attracted to

thin women, if that's what you're asking?"

I blushed, ready to drop the subject.

"If you were hoping I was first drawn to you because of your internal goodness and intellect, I'm sorry to disappoint you," John said, "but those qualities are growing on me too."

Maybe I'd have that biscuit after all. As soon as I put the butter knife down John reached for my hand.

"You remind me of my sister," he said. "She could never believe she was a beautiful woman."

Ah, his sister. Safe ground. "You and your sister are close?"

"She was ten years younger than me so it wasn't the typical brother sister relationship. She was a shy kid who never realized her beauty. She always thought she was fat, but it wasn't true. She was beautifully rounded, but not fat. I felt very protective of her."

"It sounds to me like you're a perfect big brother." I slipped my hand from under his, pretending a need to use my napkin.

John wasn't taken in by the ploy. He smiled. "Forgive me, Margaret. I'm rushing you. You still feel like a married woman, don't you?"

I hadn't felt married when Ryan had kissed me the other night, but grateful to be handed an excuse, I agreed. "I was married to Harry for over thirty years. It does feel odd to be spending so much time with another man."

"Loyalty to your husband just proves your fine character. If Audrey had understood the value of loyalty we'd still be married."

I wanted to point out that since Audrey had died in a car accident as a young woman, a long marriage would have been impossible, but I kept my mouth shut for once.

Melancholy fell over John's face. "Like my sister and my mother, you have character and loyalty, even when people don't deserve it."

This time I was the one to reach for a hand. "I was down for so long after Harry died I forgot how good life can be. These past couple weeks I've started to feel like me again." I gave his hand a squeeze. "It hasn't been that long since you lost your mother. You have to give yourself time to recover from your loss."

He leaned toward me. "Whatever happens between us, Margaret: friendship, or if I'm lucky, something more, spending time with you is always wonderful."

#

Ruby mewed and rolled around on the kitchen floor when I got home. I picked her up and held her to my cheek. She smelled like clean laundry. She squirmed to be released and I set her on the floor and went to empty the dishwasher.

I couldn't get John off my mind.

He's had a bad year, I thought, *and he's turned to me because he needs someone to talk to. I should feel glad for the attentions of a man of John's caliber*, I told myself. He was smart, sensitive and handsome.

Maybe there was something wrong with me because I couldn't return his feelings. I wanted to think it was because I hadn't healed from losing Harry, but when I considered how Ryan's kiss made me feel, I knew it wasn't true.

Face the facts, I told myself as I sorted the silverware into compartments. *You're a tease*. Years ago that's what they called women who led a man to believe he'd eventually score, just to be wined and dined.

Was that what I was doing with John? Taking advantage? Letting him buy me meals and enjoying his attentions, not to mention his scones, with no intention of ever going to bed with him?

The right thing to do was to tell John I was only interested in friendship and the next time we ate out I'd pick up the tab.

All the soul searching gave me another insight. It was time I quit feeding Ryan. John and I were thinking along the same erroneous line, trying to win someone's heart with food.

#

"Margaret, are you home?" Karen called from the back door.

"I'm here."

"Is it happy hour? I brought fresh limes."

"Then it's happy hour. I have the rum."

"Great. I want to celebrate. I sold another house."

"Congratulations!" I set out the rum and glasses.

"I sold the Berry's ranch, and the Berry's are pretty serious about a two story in the new development."

"You're on a roll."

Karen gave the lime wedge a final squeeze and took a sip of her drink. "Besides, I've met a man."

I picked up my drink and led the way to the parlor so we could settle in for some girl talk. "Tell me everything."

"Jean Ann called and asked me to play Pinochle last night. When I got there, a cousin of Albert's was the fourth."

It took a second to get my eyeballs back in my head so I could focus. "Albert's cousin? You're in lust with Albert's cousin?"

"Isn't it ludicrous? But I swear, he's nothing like Albert."

"I don't know, Karen. You'd better think this over."

"Too late. He has a Harley and he's asked me to go to a big rally in Wisconsin next week."

A Harley? May as well keep my mouth shut.

Karen sparkled with happiness. "I've been working so many hours lately. I could use a break and I can't think of a better way to spend a long weekend than on the back of a Harley Fat Boy with my arms around the waist of a good-looking man."

Karen's happiness was contagious. I said, "Neither can I."

"You approve?"

"Yes. As long as . . . what's his name?"

"Gary Minnert. I walked here so I could tell you everything. Gary's going to pick me up. He'll be here soon. We're going for a ride."

"That's good. But I hope you'll see him a few times before you hit the road for a weekend."

"Oh Margaret, you're too cautious about love."

"I prefer to think of myself as discriminating."

"If you're too discriminating, you'll miss out on a lot of fun. What about your good-looking neighbor. He's taken you out a few times. Maybe you should consider a test drive."

"No. I've thought about it and he's not for me."

"That's the trouble. You thought about it so long you talked yourself out of what could be fun and might even lead to something special."

I looked around the room.

"Are you listening to me?" Karen asked.

"Yes, you think I think too much."
I got up and called for Ruby. "Have you seen her since you got here?"

"No, and that's odd. She always comes to say hello and get her head rubbed. You don't suppose she got out when I came through the back door?"

That was my thought too. I hoped we were wrong. I checked all her favorite hiding places, and opened all the closet doors to be sure I hadn't shut her up someplace. I opened the basement door and called her name. Nothing. I went downstairs to check the furnace room. No Ruby.

Now I was sure. My little escape artist was roaming free.

"I'm so sorry, Margaret. I wasn't watching for her."

"Don't feel bad. Ruby's smart and she's sneaky. She gets out on me all the time. Eventually she comes home."

I went to the back door and called to her. Karen stood behind, watching and listening for any signs of Ruby. "Let's walk around the house," she said.

It was nearly six, and while it was still hot out the sun wasn't as brilliant and a slight breeze stirred the air enough to make it feel cooler than it was.

I started around the house one way and Karen went the other. Ruby was territorial. She seldom went beyond her own yard and when she did it was only next door to John's. I searched the hedges, calling her name, then lay on my

THE FAT WOMAN MYSTERY

belly to look under the porch, one of
Ruby's favorite hiding places.

"Do you see her?" Karen asked.

"No." I got to my feet and brushed
my hands together to free the loose
dirt. "She's not under the porch." I
heard a car start up, and seconds later
John's little red Neon backed down his
drive. I waved him down. "Have you
seen Ruby?"

John's face said it all. He wasn't
happy to know my cat was running amuck,
but he tried for a joking tone.
"Margaret, you have to be smarter than
the cat."

I knew he was wondering why I
couldn't keep my cat contained.
Obviously the man knew nothing about
cats, but this wasn't the time to get on
his bad side.

"She could be in your garage,"
Karen said. "The side door's ajar. Can
we look?"

John agreed. I pasted on my best
smile, thanked him, and exchanged waves
as he drove off.

#

The garage windows were dull with
dust, and even with the side door open
the air was humid and still. There was
a large shelving unit along the back
wall. "She could be up there," I said.
"Ruby likes to view the world from the
highest possible position."

"There's a stepladder hanging on
the wall," Karen said. "I'll get it."

"Okay, but I'll go up. The last

SANDRA NOBLE

time you climbed a ladder I ended up
running pell-mell through Alta Grove and
falling over a dead body."
When I'd climbed high enough I
started moving neatly-labeled cardboard
storage boxes to see if Ruby was hiding
behind one. I shoved 'Mom's-
Photos/Letters,' aside and looked
behind, 'Duck Decoys' and 'Alice's
CD's.' "Ruby girl," I called.
No answer.
"Listen," Karen said. The roar of
the motorcycle was unmistakable. "It's
Gary. I'll ask him to wait until we
find Ruby."
"No, you go ahead. This isn't the
first time Ruby's gotten out and it
won't be the last. She'll come home."
"Are you sure?"
"Go."
Karen threw her arms up, weaved her
body from side to side, and sang her
version of an old Steppenwolf song, "Get
your motor runnin.' Head out on the
highway. . . ."
I laughed. If anyone were born to
be free it was Karen. "Get out of
here."
Karen gave her imaginary motorcycle
some gas and drove out of the garage.
#
I put the ladder away and left the
garage. Ruby was probably hiding in one
of John's bushes watching as I looked
for her, but I was giving up. I'd fix
myself some dinner and she'd come home
when she felt like it.

242

THE FAT WOMAN MYSTERY

After the Salmon New Orleans at
noon I had to take it easy with
calories. I fixed a big salad with a
few slivers of cheese and boiled egg
slices. I topped it with Caesar
Vinaigrette with Parmesan dressing. No
sugar, no trans fats, one carb, one gram
of saturated fat, and only sixty
calories for two tablespoons.

I ate my salad with eight Thin
Crisp Triscuits. All totaled the meal
was less than five hundred calories. As
long as I didn't hit the refrigerator
before bedtime I'd have a good diet day.

\#

After I cleaned up in the kitchen
the house felt quiet, especially with
Ruby being gone. Everything was fine
during the day, but since Harry's death,
about seven every evening the house got
bigger, the silence got bigger, and the
emptiness in my heart got bigger. It
makes no sense. I'd just finished the
salad a half hour ago, but I had this
unreasonable feeling that eating would
fill up all those empty spaces.

I brewed a cup of chamomile tea,
grabbed the remote, and turned the
television on. An ad for Applebee's
flashed red ripe strawberries and a
juicy big hamburger sandwich. I clicked
the remote. Pizza Hut was touting
stuffed crust pizza.

I read in some diet book to change
activities when you want to eat. The
author suggested taking a walk or
tackling a chore you've put off. I

243

decided my shoes could use some organization. I turned the TV off, checked at the back door to see if Ruby had come home, then grabbed a magic marker and went upstairs.

Shoes are a blessing for a fat woman. Finding a new dress that looks good on you for your cousin's wedding may be an impossible task, but you can always find a snazzy pair of shoes to go with old reliable, the navy blue number you keep dragging out for weddings and funerals.

I owned maybe thirty pair of shoes, maybe more. Each pair rested in their original box and the boxes were stacked neatly on shelves. Usually I opened a minimum of five boxes before finding the pair I wanted.

Using a stool to reach the top row, I checked the contents, then labeled the shoe box 'Red Slides, Brown Half Boot, Ox Blood Loafers' . . . *Alice's CDs*.

Pow! Could it be? Could Alice be John's beloved sister? I sat in my rocking chair, thoughts bouncing around in my head like the steel balls in a pinball machine. Pushing off with my toes, I soothed myself with the rhythm, trying to sort it out.

John came from California. Alice said she was going to California to live with relatives. John said his sister was ill-used by people she cared about. If Kitty was the embezzler, then Alice had certainly been mistreated.

Nothing was solid. Everything was

circumstantial. I needed more
information. I went to the north
bedroom to look down on John's house.
It was quiet.

CHAPTER TWENTY

I put fresh batteries in the
flashlight. It wasn't dark but the sun
was sinking fast.

Purposefully, like I'd been
invited, I walked to John's back door
and turned the knob. Good. John was
adopting small town habits, the door was
unlocked. I stepped into the back
entry, relieved to be out of the sight
of neighbors. I wanted to be in and out
fast, before John came home.

Steps going down to the basement
were directly ahead of me; to my left
were three steps up to the kitchen door.
I went up.

John's bedroom seemed the best
place to start. I launched my search
with his dresser. The man was nothing
if not tidy. The more I worried about
how much time I was taking the more my
hands fumbled trying to get the tee-
shirts and jockey shorts to look as
perfect as they were before I'd rifled

through everything. I wasn't looking
for anything specific, maybe a picture,
a letter, anything that would tell me if
John's Alice was Alice Crowley.

The closet was just as neat as the
dresser drawers. I stood on tiptoes to
check the shelf. There was something
there but I couldn't reach it. I looked
around the room, but didn't see anything
to stand on. I went to the kitchen for
a chair. My skin was prickling up and
down my arms and my legs felt weak as I
toted the chair to the closet and
climbed up. I wished I knew how much
time I had.

My fingers closed around a book and
I used the flashlight in the dim closet
to see what I'd found. A scrapbook. I
turned to the first page to find faded
colored photos of two blond children, a
girl on a swing, and a much older boy
pushing her. Probably John and his
sister, but was she Alice?

I flipped through the pages. The
kids grew older toward the end of the
book, but I couldn't identify either of
them for sure.

#

I heard the car first and then
peeked around the closet door in time to
see flashes of red from the Neon's tail
lights.

Heaven save me.

John was home. *What to do, what to
do?* I tossed the scrapbook back on the
shelf, jumped off the chair and dragged
it back to the kitchen. I did a little

panicky dance, covering my mouth to
smother the urge to squeak.

Settle down, I told myself. *All
you have to do is get to the basement
then slip out the back door later, when
it's safe.*

The Neon's door slammed. I flew
down the basement and hid under the
steps, back flat against the basement
wall, breathing raggedly. I listened as
the backdoor opened.

*Don't come down. Please don't come
down.*

My heart pounded like the tell-tale
heart in Poe's classic story. Could he
hear it?

When John's footfall sounded on the
steps going up to the kitchen, I sunk to
the floor in relief.

"Meow."

Did I imagine it? My eyes
searched the shadows for Ruby. Had she
snuck in with John just now or had she
been there all along? I got to my feet,
came out from behind the steps, and
looked around.

The basement was divided by cement
block walls into several rooms. The
room at the bottom of the steps had a
washer and drier and, toward the back, a
few rugs hung from a clothesline.
Everything was clean and tidy, unlike my
own basement which grew haunted house-
sized cobwebs in record time.

"Meow."

It had come from my right. I
crossed in front of the steps and

entered a storage room. There were
boxes stacked two and three high along
the west wall. Three open boxes, with
newspaper spilling over the tops, sat in
front of the stacks, a lawn chair
nearby. It looked like John had been
searching for something.

Ruby loves playing in boxes. I
used the flash light to check out the
nearest container. Black lettering
declared the contents "Bake ware." John
had probably looked for something to
bake the scones in.

I heard Ruby's paws rapidly
scratching against cardboard, the rustle
of newspaper, and a short mew. I
focused the flashlight on another open
box several feet away. Ruby's round
yellow eyes glinted as she peeked over
the side of a medium-sized carton.
Holding my breath, praying she wouldn't
think it was a game and take off, I
crossed the room and scooped her up.
She settled into the crook of my arm
like a baby heavy with sleep.

As I soothed Ruby I slowly scanned
the contents of her box. The light
haloed a photo that Ruby's antics had
uncovered. A brass frame protected an
eight by ten high school graduation
picture of a dimpled blue-eyed blonde
girl with Farah Fawcett hair. I picked
it up, carefully inspecting her smiling
face. She looked a little like John but
most of all she looked like the woman
who'd been charged with stealing money
from the school, Alice Crowley.

I held Ruby in one arm and tucked the picture under the other. All I wanted now was to get me and Ruby safely out of John's basement. I heard a noise on the next level. John was moving through the house again. It sounded like he was directly overhead.

Ruby's eyes were narrow slits, her body vibrating with a contented purr. I held her close. Aware of each tiny squeak, I climbed the stairs to the landing and stood motionless, listening. My opportunity came guised as a flushing toilet. Using the roar of the flush for cover I slipped out the back door.

#

I called Ryan first thing. Deputy Benninga said he was in Waterloo and due back in an hour. I asked him to have Ryan stop by as soon as possible.

Alice's picture was still tucked under my arm and suddenly it felt like a hot potato. I stashed it under the Davenport and gave a little shiver. Stepping back I checked to be sure it was completely hidden.

Breathe, I told myself. I took a deep breath through my nose, held it five seconds, and then blew softly through my mouth. After I repeated it several times I went to the kitchen to brew a mug of chamomile tea.

Finally, curled in Harry's recliner, I felt calm enough to process my thoughts about Alice Crowley and the fact that she was John's sister. John must've known Alice was unbalanced.

He'd probably come to Alta Grove looking
for her. A wave of sadness swept
through me.

My heart went out to John. He
loved his sister and he was trying to
protect her. But when Alice killed
Grant he should've recognized how deeply
disturbed she was. If he'd gone to Ryan
then, he would've saved two lives. As
sorry as I felt for John's situation I
couldn't condone it. Alice had to be
stopped and Cindy exonerated.

#

The doorbell rang. Ryan was here.
I looked at the clock. He must have
finished in Waterloo sooner than he
thought he would. I had the door
partially opened before I realized.

It wasn't Ryan.

My voice croaked when I said hello
to John. *For God's sake Margaret*, I
told myself. Calm down. He has no idea
you've been in his house. I held the
door just wide enough I could put my
head out. "I'd invite you in but I know
how sick Ruby makes you. It's even
worse than usual because I haven't had
time to vacuum today. Your allergies
would go haywire." I was babbling like
an idiot.

John took hold of the door, pushed
it wide, and stepped inside. He gave me
a wan smile. "My allergies are already
haywire. I went to my basement to run a
load of laundry. My eyes started to
burn. I couldn't stop sneezing. I knew
Ruby was out and thought she might have

been in the basement."

"Oh no, I found her right after you left. She's here with me now."

"Don't lie, Margaret. While I was looking for your cat in the storage room I realized I'd had a break in."

My knees nearly gave out. I hung tight to the wall. Through sheer determination I kept my voice strong. "I'm sorry, John. With your allergies kicking up like they are, maybe it was Ruby. She's such a little Houdini. She must have slipped in when you left and out again when you got home. I hope she didn't do any damage."

"Ruby was in the house, and my sister's photo is gone." He smiled with his usually lush lips stretched thin. "We both know Ruby didn't carry the picture out of the basement."

Each time John encroached farther into the house I backpedaled until I stood in the center of the doorway that led from the foyer to the living room. John took another step, closing the distance between us, and I gave way. "You must feel terrible, knowing a stranger was going through your things."

"Margaret, I doubt very much the intruder was a stranger. It was you. You went inside looking for Ruby and while you were in the basement you started snooping. For once I'm grateful for my allergies. If I hadn't started sneezing who knows how long it would've taken me to realize the photo was gone."

I put a hand on my chest. "You're

right. I was too embarrassed to tell you. I did go after Ruby and I did see your sister's picture. She is such a sweet-looking girl. I can understand why you love her so much."

"Don't pretend, Margaret. Alice hadn't changed that much. I'm sure you recognized her. One thing I've always admired about you is your intelligence."

He took another step toward me. I saw the knife he was holding at his side and my body went weak. John reached out to steady me. "Oh my heaven, John, put that knife away. You're scaring me."

His voice was grim. "I can't tell you how sorry I am. I really like you, Margaret. You're someone very special. But I'm not going to prison. Not even for you."

I was rattled. My words seemed to run together. "John, please put the knife down. You don't have to hurt me. I'm sure you won't go to prison. No one's going to blame you for loving your sister. I just wish you'd gone to the sheriff sooner, before she killed Del and Kitty."

He threw back his head and laughed. When he stopped laughing there was still a twinkle in his eye.

"Maybe I've given your intelligence too much credit, Margaret."

He brought the knife up under my chin. I thought of Grant, staring at the stars with empty eyes, knife in his throat.

"I want that photo," John spat.

"We can talk this out. The last thing I want is to see you in prison, John."

Tears sprang up in his eyes. I wasn't sure if the tears were for me or just his allergies. *Think*, I told myself. *Keep him talking until you can find a way to save yourself.* "I know Alice didn't run around killing innocent people," I said. I know what they did to her."

"You don't know nearly as much as you think you do."

"No, I do. I know Alice didn't embezzle money from the school. I know Kitty framed her and I know Grant should have defended her instead of having her plead guilty. It must have been awful for your sister, not being able to convince anyone of her innocence."

John's eyes were red-rimmed from Ruby's dander. He wiped the allergy-induced tears from his face. "Her weak-kneed husband left her," he said. "Her friends deserted her. At that point she didn't even have faith I'd believe her. She didn't tell me anything about it until it was over and done with."

"You would've helped if you'd known how much trouble she was in."

"Every cent Alice had went to restitution and Grant Waveland's bill." His face twisted as he held off a sneeze. "When Alice showed up on my doorstep she was a broken woman with no place else to go."

His face contorted again but this

time the sneeze flew."

I saw the flash of the knife in the lamp light. *Keep him talking until Ryan gets here, it's your only chance*, I told myself. "We were all shocked when she plead guilty. I should have known Alice wasn't capable of theft. I've thought about her a lot since Cindy was arrested. I'm ashamed I didn't show her a little kindness."

John raised an eyebrow over a bloodshot eye. "Too late now, Margaret. Where did you put the picture?"

"John, you're wrong. It isn't too late to help Alice. We can find her a great lawyer. Alice doesn't belong in jail. She belongs in a hospital. Tell the sheriff where she is so she doesn't get hurt." John tilted his head and seemed to consider what I'd said. I pushed on. "They'll find her eventually, the county sheriff, the Waterloo police, the state police. They're all looking for her now."

A smile lit up his face, making his blood-rimmed eyes evil in the lamp light. "And they'll discover Alice is dead."

I felt the blood drain from my face. John giggled.

"She killed herself. Took a whole bottle of sleeping pills and washed them down with bourbon."

I was struck mute.

"Surprised?" John asked. "I don't know why, considering the way this friendly little town treated her. You all loved the gossip didn't you? Loved having something, anything, happen to relieve the deadly boredom. Alice never had a chance. The people in this town may as well have stoned her to death."

John. The man I'd shared meals with, the man I'd kissed at my back door, John was a killer.

He pressed the knife to my throat. "Everything's in place. If they ever do figure out Alice was my sister it'll be too late. I'll be in Mexico, long gone from Alta Grove."

I was the only one who knew John was Alice's brother. It didn't take a genius to realize that once John had the photo I'd be a dead woman. I finally found my voice. "John. You won't get away with this. You've killed three people." Then I thought about his wife, the unfaithful young woman who'd died along with her lover in the car wreck. "Audrey," I said out loud. "You fixed the brakes. You killed her too?"

"See," he said with a lunatic smile. "You can get away with murder. If the San Francisco police couldn't catch me, what makes you think these country bumpkins will have any better luck?

"Ryan's no bumpkin."

He removed the knife from my throat and took a step back. "Get the photo. Now."

Scratch scratch. Scratch scratch.

John's puffy eyes darted toward the couch. Ruby's sweet face appeared from under the Davenport skirt, then disappeared again. *Scratch, scratch, scratch.*

"Get that damn cat out of here or I'll kill her."

We heard the scratching again, but this time there was a different timber and I realized Ruby's claws were scraping against the glass of Alice's picture. I dropped to my knees, but before I could drag Ruby from beneath the couch, a corner of the frame emerged.

"Well, what do you know?" John grinned. "I think I'm changing my mind about Ruby. Pick it up."

I hesitated and John jabbed toward me with the knife. "Get it," he said.

I moved carefully, trying to stay out of striking range, and pulled the picture from its hiding place. My hands were shaking so much I nearly dropped the heavy brass frame. Ruby emerged as I got to my feet.

"Meow," she said in protest of having her plaything taken from her.

John started taking short little breaths as a sneeze built in his chest. He put a finger to his nose but the sneeze continued to build. "Ahhh . . . Ahh . . ."

His head went back then slammed forward. As the KaChoooo ripped through his body, I raised Alice's picture and brought it crashing down on his head. Glass flew everywhere and the knife fell from John's hand. I scooped it up and ran like hell.

I hit the front door like a
battering ram and flew down the porch
steps, my mind whirling, trying to come
up with an escape route. The car. I
heard his footfall behind me. The foyer
light was on and John was lit from
behind. I tried to scream to draw
someone's attention but night had fallen
and the mosquitoes had driven everyone
inside to sit in front of their
televisions. There was no one to hear
the pathetic little squeak that caught
in my throat.

He was coming. I'd never make it
to the car. John held his head with one
hand and weaved a little coming down the
porch steps. Could I make it across the
street to the neighbors? A surge of
adrenalin released me from fear and
indecision.

Without a thought to traffic I
darted into the street in front of a
motorcycle. The bike bore down on me.
With the strength of the bionic woman I
leaped to evade its path.

My feet slid out from under me as I
hit pavement and I landed on my butt,
coughing and sputtering from the bike's
exhaust. John stood across the street,
his bloody face ghastly in the
illumination of the streetlight. I saw
the beginnings of a smile as he stepped
toward me. The man had nothing left to
lose.

As I scrambled to my feet, I heard
the roar of the motorcycle. He was

coming back. John stopped, his face contorted in frustration, and then he retreated into the darkness of my yard.

#

The motorcycle driver wore black leather chaps and a black leather vest with a tight black Harley Tee-shirt that defined bulging biceps. He took his helmet off and shook out dark shoulder length hair. There was something familiar about him.

"Are you alright?" he asked.

"If I don't have a heart attack in the next few minutes, I think I'll survive."

He shook his head. "It was a close one. I was scared." He grinned, "Hell, I guess I'm still scared.

I nearly laughed when it dawned on me who the motorcycle driver was. "You're Albert's cousin, aren't you?"

#

Gary Minnert helped me inside and called the police. He was picking gravel from my hand when Ryan arrived.

"I was wrong about Alice," I said. She didn't kill anyone. "She's dead."

"I know. Her parole officer told me she'd gone to San Francisco. We checked the death records when we couldn't find an address."

"John Gildenbond is her brother." As quickly as I could I told him about the photo and my escape from John. "If Gary hadn't decided to come back to check on me I don't think I'd be here right now."

"I saw him take off," Gary said. "He was headed south."

"I'll get on the radio and call the state police," Ryan said. "Will you take Margaret to Karen's?"

I protested. "I'll be just fine right here."

Ryan threw his hands in the air. "Maggie, for once just do what I ask so I can do my job without worrying about you?"

CHAPTER TWENTY-ONE

One Hundred and ninety-eight pounds
was my official naked before breakfast,
after using the bathroom, early morning
weight.

The Fit Girls were gathered in my
parlor. We were holding an afternoon
meeting. Karen and Gary were taking a
weekend trip on his motorcycle and Sara
and Bruce were leaving the kids with her
parents so they could spend a couple
days with friends in Davenport. The
girls thought a meeting might keep them
strong in the face of temptation while
they were away.

"I've broken the two hundred pound
barrier and hit the wonderful ones," I
said.

Sara and Karen clapped and cheered
for me.

"You're amazing," Sara said. "I'm
thrilled for you." Her face was
shining, she was so beautifully sincere
in her happiness for me.

Karen crossed the room and gave me

a hug. "You've turned the corner. I know it's been hard since Harry died, but you're on your way back now."

For the first time I let them see my tears. "Yes. Losing Harry was the worst thing to ever happen to me. I can't tell you how hard it's been."

Sara crossed the room to hug me too. "We know."

Of course they knew. I looked tough to the rest of the world but the twenty pounds I'd gained spoke volumes to the Fit Girls. They knew I'd been wearing my pain.

"That's enough hugging and crying," I said. "I'd celebrate dropping out of the two hundreds, but my first inclination for a celebration is to go out to eat."

"That won't do. But we could make a list of little rewards," Karen suggested.

Sara jumped on the idea. "Yes. Like you've wanted that new Andrea Bocelli CD. Or you could get a pedicure."

"Margaret needs something big. She's out of the two hundreds. She needs a reward worthy of the feat."

"I don't know how she's going to top solving a murder," Sara said.

"That's for sure," Karen agreed. "Say, just how did Ryan pick John up so fast?"

"Score one for the country bumpkins," I said. "The blood trail from John's head wound led them to the

house behind mine where Max Vinton's
Buick was missing. They called it in,
and the highway patrol nabbed John
before he could get out of McCall
county."

"Why did the killer have to be a
good-looking single man?" Karen asked.
"For a while I thought you two were
hitting it off."

Sara agreed. "He did seem taken
with you Margaret."

"After I found Grant's body, and
especially after John learned Ryan and I
were old friends, I think he
deliberately cultivated a relationship
so he could stay close to the
investigation."

"Maybe," Karen said, "But I think
it was more than that."

"What? You think I should send
letters to the man in prison? Maybe be
one of those freaks who marries the
lifer?"

"Of course not," Karen said.

Sara spoke in a conciliatory tone.
"I think Karen's just thinking it's time
you consider a relationship."

The whole conversation was putting
me on edge. I was afraid they'd start
in on Ryan next, and I didn't want to
tell them I hadn't heard from him since
the night John was arrested.

Karen wouldn't drop the subject.
"So John wasn't the right guy."

"You act like the problem was
something like he's a Catholic and I'm
Jewish. For heaven's sake the man's a

killer," I said with more zeal than
necessary.

"Don't be upset with us," Sara
said. "All we're saying is it's time to
consider romance."

Karen grinned. "What? Are you
ready to give sex up?"
#
The girls left around five in the
afternoon. I was considering a nap when
the phone rang. I debated whether or
not to answer. It was really too late
to nap if I wanted to sleep tonight. I
went to the phone.

It was Cindy. "Ryan came by. All
the charges against me have been
dropped."

"Fantastic. You must feel like a
million bucks."

Ryan said you hit John Gildenbond
over the head with a framed photo and
that's why they found him. I want to
thank you, Margaret. I really think I
might have ended up in prison if it
hadn't been for you."

"Ryan's a better sheriff than that.
He would have figured it out."

"Maybe. Another thing, Margaret, I
can't tell you how wonderful it is to
know Grant wasn't having an affair with
Kitty. Things weren't perfect with us,
as you know, but I really think we would
have worked it out."

"Of course you would've."
Uncomfortable with her praise, I changed
the subject. "How's the diet going?
Are you still baking cookies?"

Cindy laughed. "I've been so upset since Grant was killed I haven't been able to eat. I've lost five pounds."

"Good for you," I said. What I was thinking was less generous. Why is it some people stop eating when they're stressed? Not me. The more stress I feel, the more I eat. I don't even stop eating when I have a cold and my food's tasteless. I keep searching for that magic something that will taste good. Something that will make me feel better.

I tuned into Cindy again.

"I called home to let my parents know the charges have been dropped," she said, "and they suggested I move back to Des Moines. I think I'm going to do it."

I wasn't surprised. A lot of people in Alta Grove were happy to believe Cindy had killed her husband. They liked the idea of one of the beautiful people being cut down to size. If I were Cindy, this town would be a good place to put behind me. I love Alta Grove, and believe me, there are a million good reasons to live here, but I'm not blind to our faults.

"I'll miss you," I said, "but it'll be nice for you to have your family near, and they'll be a lot of help raising Angie."

#

John's revenge had harmed a lot of innocent people. Not just Angie and Cindy, but Kitty's parents, Del's girlfriend, and even the town. When I

allowed myself to consider it, I
realized I'd been hurt too. John's
attentions were fun. His flirtations
made me feel vibrant. Sometimes I'd
even believed Ryan was interested and it
was a pretty heady feeling to think two
men found me desirable.

Now I understood John's unsavory
reasons for keeping me near, and as for
Ryan, he hadn't bothered to call. Karen
had a new love interest. She'd be
scarce until her infatuation for Gary
ran its course or she married him,
whichever came first. Sara had Bruce,
now and forever.

*Oh, for heaven's sake, shake it
off*, I told myself. *You don't even want
to be married again. You're just
wallowing in self-pity. Pull yourself
together and make the best of the
evening.*

I checked the television schedule.
At seven the classic movie channel was
showing North by Northwest. I love Cary
Grant and I hadn't seen North by
Northwest in years. First I'd rid
myself of my nasty bra and give the
dents in my shoulders a chance to spring
back. Before the movie there'd be
plenty of time for a soak in the tub.

\#

While I sat in the tub I planned
dinner. I had a small New York Strip
steak in the refrigerator, and a bag of
organic spring greens for a salad.
Maybe I'd open a can of organic peas
too. Where were those old TV trays?

I sank deep into the claw foot tub and relaxed. The phone rang but for once I ignored it. *Let the answering machine pick up.* When the water cooled I flipped the hot water lever with my toes and heated it up again. Showers are so overrated. Finally, I washed my hair, shaved my legs, and even remembered to run the razor over my chin.

#

I had a new attitude. Fresh smelling and dressed in my Disney princess PJ's, I bounded down the stairs. I was hungry and looking forward to my steak and watching Cary Grant and Eva Marie Saint flirt on the train.

Just as the George Foreman Grill was hot, the front doorbell rang. Before I could get to the foyer I heard the front door shut and Ryan's voice as he stepped inside.

"Maggie? Are you here?"

"I'm here." My upper arms prickled with goose bumps. I met him in the foyer. Ryan was in tan Dockers and a salmon pink collared polo shirt. I sucked in a bit of drool and bit my lower lip.

"I called earlier but you didn't answer, so I took a chance and came by."

"I was in the tub." My words were measured. I looked at him, trying to read the purpose of the visit. The blue of his eyes was so dark they were unfathomable, but his smile was warm.

"I owe you dinner," he said. I was
hoping we could go someplace nice,
someplace we could talk, but if you want
to stay in your pajamas I guess we could
go to Waterloo and drive through
McDonalds or Burger King."
"I'll get dressed."

THE FAT WOMAN MYSTERY

ABOUT THE AUTHOR

Sandra Noble lives in Iowa with her cat, Beulah. While Sandra
has lived in Iowa for many years, she has also lived in Alaska,
Colorado, and Washington. She has published short stories
and essays in magazines, but The Fat Woman Mystery is
Sandra's first novel. She is now working on a second Fat
Woman book.

CPSIA information can be obtained at www.ICGtesting.com
Printed in the USA
LVOW05s1216180214

374190LV00014B/267/P